The Castle Ghosts

a novella by Ashleen O'Gaea

All rights reserved under the Pan-American and International Copyright Conventions. This book may not be reproduced in whole or in part by any means electronic or mechanical, including photocopying, recording, or by any information storage, retrieval, or distribution system now known or hereafter invented, without written permission from the copyright holder ... except for short quotes used in reviews.

This is a work of fiction. Most names, characters, places and incidents are either the product of my imagination or are used fictitiously (or favorably). Any significant resemblance to actual persons/lives is coincidental. That includes what Father Michael has to say about Catholic theology.

Wicca is a real religion; the spells in this book were created for this story. Fifth-wheel trailers are obviously real, and so are some of the Kampgrounds of America, various restaurants and pubs the protagonist enjoys, and the Facebook pages where she connects with other people who vacation or live in RVs.

Copyright 2020 by Ashleen O'Gaea
Coyote Song Publishing

ONE

Anonymous isn't a necessity, just my preference. I'm not completely off the grid, but I'm as close as you can get and still have a driver's license.

"A woman's home is her castle," they say, so that's what I named the fifth-wheel trailer I live in. In keeping with its name, I put a six-inch gargoyle in a corner of the shelf above the china hutch. The Castle is thirty-four feet long. Like the hidden gargoyle, it almost disappears if I park it between a forty-five foot diesel-pusher and a forty-eight foot fiver.

My truck's pretty ordinary, too. A used Ford with a couple of bangs and scratches, like me. I scraped the side of the fiver with the pick-up's mirror the first time I parked next to it, too, so nothing looks new.

The Castle is comfortable, big enough that I can keep my work and my pleasure separate, and small enough that I don't feel lost or lonely. It's fully equipped, and I can use what I want to when I want to. It makes for the nice anonymous life I like.

I have a few live, in-person friends, but no social media accounts. It's with one of those in-person friends that this story starts.

Marianne lives in London, going on a decade now. I met her in high school. I was the girlfriend she went to the movies with after bad break-ups with the geniuses and jocks. People thought she looked fast and easy, but she wasn't; hence the bad break-ups.

Every Christmas she sends me a card, enclosing a few pictures. I don't celebrate Christmas myself. Mid-Winter's my holiday, even if I am pretty casual about it. But last Christmas, for the first time ever, Marianne sent me a present.

It was a box, an antique box. I liked it. It wasn't decorated, except for a stained carving on the top. It seemed to be right at home in The Castle.

Then, before I'd let myself really enjoy her gift, I had to go find something to send to her. That took weeks, because she has a classier life than I do, and I didn't want to send her anything I could find where I usually shop. That's why it was spring before I found time to really look at the box.

I reread the card she'd sent with it.

Seelie, it said, *the man at the shop said this is a Victorian puzzle box, but my friend Meryl says its an enclosed secret drawer, and much older, from maybe the Renaissance. I'm not sure why it made me think of you, but it did, so here it is. Merry Christmas!*

I knew that puzzle boxes – sometimes called maze boxes – developed in Victorian times from the Renaissance idea of secret compartments in furniture, but I didn't know much else. If Marianne's friend Meryl says it might date from the Renaissance, that's good enough for me. Maybe as early as the thirteen hundreds, maybe from the sixteens. It's a present; I wasn't researching it.

The symbol carved in the top of the box looked like some fancy monogram. Or maybe it was some kind of creature on it – hard to tell, at least for me, with only what I've learned from *Antiques Roadshow* to give me an idea.

Sometimes the design looked like an animal, but the carving was chipped with time and so encrusted with grime I thought I might do more harm than good to clean it. I put the different ways it looked down to the way I held it and the light, and didn't give it much serious thought.

I'd just gotten settled at a favorite campground up in northern Arizona. It was raining – yeah, it does do that in Arizona – so instead of sitting outside with a bourbon, I sat inside with one. And decided to see if I could open the puzzle box. It took some patience, but the bourbon helped with that.

After about an hour of turning, eyeballing, poking, pushing, prying with my fingernails and whatnot, I had it open. There was something inside.

It was a small packet of oiled cloth. It still had some scent to it, but I wasn't sure what it smelled like. The string around it was partly gone, so it wasn't hard to open. What it wrapped was a lock of hair, in a ring.

The ring looked like amethyst to me. It was deep purple, flat in the middle, and beveled on the sides. Its setting was gold, and it was a little bent – but gold's malleable, and if the box really was six hundred years old, a dent or two might be expected.

I could get it on my right ring finger, but I don't wear gold. I thought about sending it to Marianne. It looked like the kind of thing she might wear, and her birthday was, if I remembered right, in February. Amethyst's her birthstone.

But I didn't. I sent her a garden sculpture of a saguaro cactus, because I was in Arizona for the next few months, and people in England seem to like Wild West stuff. So I put the ring back in the box, with the lock of hair – blonde - and left it open. I did go so far as to move it from the end of the kitchen island to one of the side tables at the ends of the couch, under a lamp so the amethyst would glitter a little.

For a couple of days, nothing happened. And then I started hearing the singing.

TWO

The Baroness Cecelya deHulle died in 1405, surrounded by her family.

There were windows on the east and west sides of her chamber, so at ten in the morning it was light. Cecelya looked peaceful, and the chamber was quiet, except for the soft crying of Cecelya's six-year-old niece, Gwenda Willoughby.

Daughter of Cecelya's late sister Elisot, Gwenda spent part of every spring with her father's family, and the rest of the year with the deHulles. Unusual though it was, the arrangement suited everyone, especially her father, William, and his too-soon-married second wife, Olive.

Cecelya's daughter, Margaret, rested her hands on her cousin's shoulders, hoping to comfort her. No one made any effort to still the girl's thin, mournful voice. Her grief was real; Cecelya and Gwenda were close. If Cecelya's fourth daughter had lived, she'd have been Gwenda's age, and Margaret thought of her as another sister.

The window to the west bed was open for Cecelya's soul, and the curtains stirred slightly in the breeze. The light changed just enough to make Cecelya's hair look lighter than it was ... and to let Margaret notice the box that Gwenda was clutching.

She knew what it was. It was the puzzle box – maze box, Cecelya called it – that the Baroness had given to Gwenda last Christmas. It came from Italy. It was the secret drawer of a dresser, with a thin frame built around it.

Fifteen-year-old Margaret had enjoyed the story Cecelya told Gwenda about the box. The five year-old had listened raptly.

"There was a great ship bringing the dresser over from far across the sea," she'd said. "But a storm came up and sank the ship, and all the sailors got away, but they couldn't save the cargo.

"Then mermaids found it all, and in thanks for the bounty – because mermaids are always looking for furniture that isn't made of shells, you know – they took out the secret drawer and made it into a box, and cast it up on the shore.

"They wrote your name on a little shell, and tied it on with seaweed. And when your father, William, found it, he brought it right home."

"But then he had to go away again, and so he left the maze box with you for me?"

"That's right, darling," Cecelya said.

If Cecelya knew where the box had really come from, or what happened to the dresser it was probably from, she never said anything about it. The pleasant story softened Olive's rejection of the little girl, which William did little to mitigate. Gwenda loved her mermaid's maze box, and most days carried it with her everywhere.

Margaret thought she might put a lock of her mother's golden hair, only just touched with a bit of grey, in the box for

Gwenda to keep. But they'd wait, until they were sure Cecelya's soul had crossed over.

Margaret was the only other person who knew that Cecelya might expect to rest in the Summerland rather than in Heaven. She went through the motions and spoke the words of Catholicism, but once in the month, when the Moon was full ....

Margaret thought dancing with witches was her mother's only secret, and she kept it well, and forever. Apostacy was a mortal sin, and by Margaret's reckoning, Cecelya wasn't the least bit sorry.

Margaret wasn't sure how she felt about her silence. She thought she probably ought to confess her mother's sin, but .... The Fourth Commandment bid her honor her mother and father; surely trusting Cecelya was the right thing to do.

Margaret felt sure that her mother was meeting with witches, but the Eighth Commandment was to never bear false witness. And Cecelya did still go to chapel and recited all the prayers. Margaret's conscience decided to give her mother the benefit of the doubt, and she said nothing

Was her mother's death God's punishment for her witchcraft? Margaret considered this, and thought perhaps not. There was no reason to disbelieve the doctor, who said it was bad mushrooms. One of the scullery maids must have made a mistake, and she had been chastised and given a heavy penance, but not otherwise punished. Baron deHulle thought to honor his wife by mercy for her death.

Now, instead of trying to silence Gwenda's weeping, her nurse Winfrith started to sing, very softly. After one or two more sniffles, Gwenda's tender soprano joined Winfrith's alto - and her cousin's flat tones - in the words to Auntie Cecelya's favorite hymn.

●

"I want to leave the box here tonight," Gwenda told Margaret. "It makes it easier for me to sleep, so I thought it might help Auntie Cecelya, too. Do you think that's alright?"

"I think that's very sweet," Margaret managed to say. She had a lot on her mind. With her father still at least a day's ride away, and her older sisters in France, it was up to Margaret to see to most of the arrangements.

Of course the clerics wanted to take over, and Margaret did not want to let them. She would hide what she thought was her mother's true faith, but Margaret had dreamed last night, and knew what she must do.

In the dream, an old woman came to her, and whispered about certain herbs, and told her what words she must hold in her heart for Cecelya. On the next full Moon, the dream-hag told Margaret, she should go to the woods ....

Margaret had no idea what she was to do in the woods; she had woken in terror, enough of the dream still with her that she could see the witch's shadow and smell the mice that were her familiars.

She did her best to put the dream out of her mind, and not to imagine her mother burning in Hell forever. She would never tell anyone – and she would not go to the woods, not ever, no matter what the phase of the Moon.

Now, there were mourners to be hired – she could delegate that, at least – and the wake to be organized. Margaret wanted to do that herself, to be sure that none of the herbs the dream-witch had mentioned flavored the foods that would be served.

The priest could lead the prayers through the night, and Margaret would sit with him so as not to think of her mother's sisters-in-belief in the woods, for she imagined they were conducting their own memorial rituals.

Despite her fear, Margaret almost wished she could bring herself to meet those women in the woods, attend one of those rites for which her mother had risked her immortal soul. But she was afraid. She needed the priest's prayers as much as her mother did.

With Margaret's absent-minded permission, Gwenda left her mermaid box on one of the tables, beside a candle. They found in the morning that wax had dripped on it, but when one of the ladies wanted to clean it off, Gwenda raised a fuss.

"No harm," Margaret said when she was consulted. "Leave it be."

When Cecelya's Will was read, it turned out that she had left a bequest for Gwenda: two amethysts, one in a ring and one on a chain. Her fingers were too small for the ring, so Gwenda wrapped it, and the lock of Cecelya's hair she got from Margaret, in oiled cloth and tucked it into the maze box.

Years later, when the funeral wax was dry and brittle and cracked off the lid of the box, it seemed to Gwenda that the wax stain looked like a mermaid; that's what she told her daughter it was. "That's the very mermaid who gave this to my father for me."

Even more years later, Gwenda's granddaughter's husband carved a curlie-cue mermaid over the stain. The box became a family heirloom, and that that there was a ring and a lock of hair hidden inside was forgotten. Sometime in the middle of Victoria's reign, during a clearing out, the old, stained and crudely carved box was found and set out for sale. It brought twelve pence.

In the nineteen-seventies, an antique dealer found it in a small trunk he'd bought, unopened at the time of the auction, for five pounds. When he saw it, he recognized it as a puzzle box, but – and he couldn't have said why if anyone had asked him – he didn't put it out to sell. When his daughter inherited the shop in the 'nineties, she never noticed it in the dusty back room. Her son, however, saw it and set it out on a curio shelf. It sat for several years, but eventually, Marianne Holmes saw it out of the corner of her eye.

For some reason, it reminded her of her friend Seelie Ames. They didn't exchange gifts, just ... winter cards, because Seelie's was always late for Christmas. But Marianne's feeling was strong, so for three pounds she bought the box. It cost her more than that to send it to Seelie, and she didn't care.

A few weeks later, her friend sent something back, a large but relatively lightweight box. The note with the metal cactuses - lightly rusted, with only the saguaro's blossom painted, white and yellow – was in Seelie's almost Copperplate hand.

Marianne, it said, *thanks for the box. It looks great in The Castle, and I love looking at the sort of carving thing on the top. Haven't opened it yet – saving that for a rainy day. Hope you like the saguaro. Happy birthday!*

THREE

It might have been Latin, the singing.

It was mostly droning, but one high pitched voice stood out. It wasn't enough to identify any words, not that I'd understand Latin, if that's what it was. It sounded mournful, though.

I wasn't dreaming. I thought I might have been, at first, but no, that was not the explanation. And I do not sleep with my radio on, and don't have it tuned to any stations that might play Latin (as distinct from Latino) music.

By the time I got out of bed, turned on a couple of lights, and cocked my ear in all three of my rooms (three counting the bathroom), and decided it was coming from the living room, it had stopped. I put it down to a strange case of tinnitus, and went back to bed.

Three nights later, it happened again. This time I didn't turn on any lights. I have an LED night light in the bathroom, so I just opened the door a little, so I could see my stairs, and went right down into the living room. I'd been thinking about it, of course, and had started to piece an idea together.

Latin (probably) chanting. Renaissance or older box. Unlikely as it seemed that a box would be chanting, I thought there might be some connection. Had I released something from it? Was there a ... a ghost song attached to the ring, or the lock of hair?

If only it had been that simple.

•

In some of the places I park The Castle, there are lights throughout the park. In Arizona they're usually sodium lights, those sort of peachy-colored ones that don't interfere too much with night-sky viewing. The Castle has black-out curtains throughout, so if I'm parked under a lamp, I can still sleep in the dark.

That's why it seemed odd to me that there was a soft golden glow in the living room. It was probably there the first night I heard the singing, but with the lights on, I didn't notice it. That second night, I noticed it.

There's the little red light from the fireplace, to show you if it's on or off, and from the right angle, you can see it reflected on the floor, but it doesn't cast a glow throughout the room.

There's a little green light at the other end of the island; it's the CO monitor, and the light lets you know its battery is good to tell you if there's a leak. It doesn't cast a glow either. None of the equipment lights do.

It was mist-like, the glow, and very faint. If not for the black-out curtains, I'd never have noticed.

"Hello?"

I don't normally speak to mists or glows, and I spoke without giving it much thought. It didn't vocalize in response, but it did seem to shimmer a little. Was that an answer?

When I'm staying somewhere with cable, and I can find them without a TV guide, I'll watch those ghost-hunting shows.

I think it would be fun to explore a haunted house, but it never occurred to me that I might need any spirit-detecting gizmos myself. I grant you that a lot of old European castles are haunted, but I never thought mine would be.

I do, however, have flashlights. I got one out, loosened the lens housing a little so it wouldn't take much to turn it on, and set it on the counter. It works for some of the TV ghost hunters, so I thought I might as well give it a try.

"Hello?" I said again. "If you can understand me, see if you can turn on this light. It should work if you can just touch it."

I thought I saw the shimmer again, and then the flashlight came on. After that, the glow disappeared. Hmm.

If I'm a ghost from the fifteenth century, and I touch a stick and it lights up without flame, I'm going to be a little freaked out, I thought. So I said, "It's not magic. It's not dangerous. It's just a machine. It won't hurt you, and neither will I."

In about five seconds, the glow came back, slowly, and I had another idea. I went to the box and got the ring. "Is this your ring?" I asked, setting it on the counter where the flashlight had been.

The glow collected itself and comet-tailed into the amethyst, almost like Jeannie smoking into her bottle. I took that for a yes. But where could we go from there?

Clearly the glow – the ghost – understood me. It might have claimed the ring without my asking about it, but turning on the flashlight, that required comprehension. So – not only sentient, but able to understand English. That was good to know, but yes-or-no questions will only take you so far. I still couldn't think how I'd be able to understand anything the ghost wanted to tell me.

FOUR

There wasn't much for it but to start with yes-or-no questions, though, so that's what I did.

"I think you can understand me," I said, "so I'd like to see if we can talk to each other a little bit. If you can make the ring glow twice for 'yes' and once for 'no,' we could try. Is that alright with you?"

The ring did nothing.

"Are you afraid?" I asked.

The ring glowed, darkened, and glowed again.

"You're not where you expected to be, are you?"

The glow pulsed in the ring.

"Did you die in England?"

A few unglowing seconds passed, and then the ring started to pulse wildly, brightly, dozens of times.

"Do you remember dying?"

The ring darkened, and stayed that way for another couple of seconds. Then it flashed once.

"I don't know what happened to you, but I can tell you how I ... found you," I said.

The ring flashed twice.

"A friend of mine lives in London. You know London?"

"Yes," the ring flashed.

"It's the year two-thousand and eighteen," I said. I expected that to take her aback a bit. I assumed the ring-energy was a female, because it was obviously a lady's ring.

"No," she pulsed.

"Yes," I said. I paused, but she didn't reject the idea again, so I went on. "My friend in London saw a puzzle box - a maze box - in a shop. She bought it and gave it to me as a present. We think it's very old. Maybe the fourteen hundreds," I added.

"Yes," she flashed.

"Fourteen hundreds?"

"Yes." A pause, and then the ring flashed "yes" again.

"Are you starting to remember?"

The ring's stone pulsed three times.

"Do you mean maybe?"

"Yes."

"The box - was it yours too?"

Her "yes" was followed a moment later by a "no."

I thought about that. Yes, it was her box, but no, it wasn't .... I had a thought. "Did you give it to somebody?"

She pulsed "yes" twice.

"And the ring?"

"Yes."

"And a lock of hair?"

"Maybe," she pulsed out.

"So ... you lived and died in England, in the fourteen hundreds, and the box and the ring were yours and you gave them to somebody."

"Yes." This was followed by a very long glow that wavered a little. "You're welcome," I said, hoping I'd guessed right about the meaning of the long glow. "Shall we rest for a while now?"

"Yes," she answered, and so we did.

•

Over the course of the next few days, our conversations punctuated by the routines of my life at the KOA where I was staying, we established quite a bit more about the energy that felt at home in the ring.

I had asked if she was a lady, and she said she was, and then it occurred to me that to a fifteenth-century woman, "lady" didn't mean just any old woman, but a titled woman. I asked if I should call her "my lady," and she said I should.

I googled again, and found out that meant that she had to have been at least a baroness. That felt like progress; it's always nice to know who the ghost is that you're communicating with. I was going to google her rank and year of death, but a pine tree came down and took some electrical lines with it, and we were out of power for a while.

This alarmed me. I do have battery power, and solar, too, but without shore power, as they call it, I can't use my lights – well, won't – and shouldn't open the 'fridge. I don't have a generator because I don't want one, even for emergencies, so that meant I was offline till shore power was restored.

We got the power back pretty quickly, but by then I had gone out and taken a walk in the almost-not-rain, and The Castle's ghost didn't blink at me when I came back in. I had things to do, so it was a few hours before I could focus on her again.

I spent that evening reading – my e-reader is always charged, and its battery is long-lasting – and the next morning was my scheduled time to grocery shop. Thus, it was not until later that day that I remembered about googling baronesses who died in the fourteen hundreds.

What I found out, after asking a few more questions and finally getting a "yes" from the ghost, is that Baroness Cecelya deHulle died on the twenty-eighth of May in 1405, in Eresby, Lincolnshire, England. It wasn't quite proper, but I finally got her to let me call her Lady Cecelya.

It should've been Lady deHulle, but I had a reason for wanting to call her Cecelya. People call me Seelie, a diminutive my Irish grandmother suggested, but it's short for Cecelya.

Yeah, spelled that way. I'd always been told it was a "weird family spelling." If not for Granny Sheila's getting the name Seelie to stick, I'd have been Cecelya too. Nobody'd ever told me where the family spelling of my name came from. My guess now is that they just didn't know, but what they said was, "Every life should have a little mystery in it."

Eventually I solved that mystery. It turned out to be perfectly reasonable to familiarize The Castle's ghost as Lady Cecelya. Some time after that, for a while, anyway, I kind of wished it wasn't.

FIVE

Whether or not your castle has a ghost, life goes on.

Floors must be swept, dishes, no matter how few, must be done and put away; shopping must be accomplished, laundry must be carted to and from the campground's facilities. (No, I don't have a washer/dryer unit in my fifth-wheel, and no, I have no plans to install one.)

Now and again I had to take care of some financial business, and even do a little work from home. So interesting as she and our new relationship was, it didn't – couldn't – take all of my time.

Sometime after the Spring Equinox, I found a way to communicate with her beyond asking questions that could be answered with "yes," "no," or "maybe." What I thought was that if I wore the ring, she might be able to channel her thoughts to my mind.

Did it occur to me that this could be dangerous? That this could be some kind of demon, waiting for an opportunity to possess me, and wreak its evil will around the countryside? No, it did not. I trusted my trust of Lady Cecelya.

But what happened was not mental telepathy with the ghost in the ring. What happened was automatic writing.

A few seconds after I slid the ring over my right-hand ring finger, I had an overwhelming urge to sit down with a paper and pen. Lady Cecelya felt a little pushy in my mind, but I supposed she was used to telling people what to do, being a baroness and all.

We had some trouble at first. Her idea of English was very different from mine. She understood me reasonably well, but her own, older, English tended to be Welsh-accented. It also took her some time to accustom herself to my writing. But after a week or so of scribbling – sometimes deliberate, to both our delights – we managed to compromise. She "told" me what to write in her broken and resentful English, and sometimes clarified with mental images, which grew stronger as time passed.

She resented English because it had been forced upon her people, a couple of generations before she was born. Her mother, Aline Walensis, was the first generation born into Edward the First's imposition of English rule on Wales. The only bright side was that people like Lady Cecelya's grandparents and parents became patrons of Welsh poets, once the princes had been essentially dethroned by the Statute of Rhuddlan.

Her ladyship – with a little help from me and the Internet – explained her understanding of history. Shropshire, where she lived and died, was originally Wales. Rebellions against the English were mounted, of course, none of which were successful. The English (she had some choice adjectives which I understood without translation) "knew they could not stand against the Welsh and the French together, so they assassinated our heroes, the ... the sice," I wrote. She corrected my spelling to sais.

"Tush teen pob sice," she added defiantly, and corrected my spelling again. *Twill tin pob sais.*

A few years before she died, though, Owain Glyndwr – whom the English dishonored by Anglicizing his name to Owen Gendower – led what history knows as the Glyndwr Rising, the last war of Welsh independence. When Cecelya died, he was still undefeated, and she still had hope.

Of course I checked this all out online, and found out that not only was I a distant descendant of Lady Cecelya's, but that Glyndwr might have been fostered, briefly, in her great-grandfather's house. My connection to the Welsh uprisings is another eighteen generations away, with not a few English ancestors thrown in, but I could still understand her being pissy about the English.

I found that if I wrote down what I wanted to say to her, it helped me concentrate enough for her to "hear" me even though I wasn't saying anything out loud. It amused her no end that I called my small house a castle.

"No stones," she said. "No arrow slits. Not a castle."

"My lady," I wrote, "in these days we say that even a commoner's home is her castle – because she is in charge of what happens within, just as you were in charge - ...."

"Not a castle," she interrupted. "But I like your gargoyle."

●

The more we chatted, the more she remembered, and the more she remembered, the more agitated she became. I had to leave the ring off for longer periods of time. It seems that one of her relatives, or one of their friends – someone she saw often – had negotiated with Owain Glyndwr, and though she could not admit it at the time, she felt the outcome as a betrayal.

On Facebook, we'd say the relationship between England and Wales was, in Cecelya's time, "complicated." Her husband's family had to chart a careful course, because the Penal Laws denied the Welsh the right to carry arms, to hold office, and to live in fortified towns. They applied to Englishmen who married Welsh women, too, so ....

But, as Cecelya pointed out, the Penal Laws weren't enacted until 1402, so any betrayal of the Welsh before that was inexcusable. Married at sixteen to William, an hereditary baron of Hulle, she had to balance her Welsh loyalty – largely secret, as was her personal faith, she hinted – with her English duties. Complicated indeed, I had to agree.

"In these times," I told her, "disagreements are resolved by voting, and nobles' votes don't carry more weight."

She considered this. "So the Welsh and the English, their votes count equally?"

"Yes," I said.

"So ... there is peace at last? And Wales is independent?"

"Sort of," I said.

By my hand, she drew a long, jagged line on the page we were using, which I took as narrow-eyed skepticism.

"The kingdom is united," I said. "It's called the United Kingdom of England and Northern Ireland, and it includes England, Northern Ireland, Scotland, and Wales. But those four are separate countries, with their own parliaments."

"They have made an alliance."

"Yes."

"And they are at peace?"

"They're not taking up arms against each other, but there are still some who are not satisfied with the terms of the alliance."

"Then perhaps not much has changed in the six hundred years you say it's been since my death."

"Six hundred thirteen," I said.

I probably wouldn't have said anything more, even if I'd known at the time, but not too much later, I really hoped some things – about Lady Cecelya – had changed a lot, because .... But I'm getting ahead of myself.

SIX

Some people don't like having ghosts in their home, and some don't mind.

I didn't mind, but maybe that was because she came in with an artifact, and wasn't trying to get me to leave my home. The Castle was too new to have its own place-ghosts.

For quite some time, it was unnecessary for me to use my awning lights at night, because if I wasn't wearing her ring, she was curious, and glowed softly when she looked out the window. Given the way some people rail about other people's lights ruining an evening's ambiance, that was convenient.

Somebody asked once what it was, the glow, and without thinking I said, "Oh, that's just Lady Cecelya on stand-by," and they chuckled and said, "Yeah, I renamed my Alexa, too."

We had some good times. It wasn't often that I wore Lady Cecelya's ring outside The Castle, so when I did, it was a real treat for both of us. I took her to the Grand Canyon once. She was a little confused by the horseless carriage, and maybe a little woozy from my hand being on the steering wheel; but she was very impressed when she saw the South Rim through my eyes.

"How deep is it?" she wondered.

"A mile," I said. Her mind felt blank. I thought for a moment. "Eight furlongs."

"Oh!" Just so you know, someone else being surprised in your mind is an odd feeling.

"And eighteen hundred and sixteen furlongs in length," I added. "It goes on beyond those twists and turns. That's more than a third the length of England."

She had nothing to say to that. She had not, I thought, been the length of England, so the comparison might not have been one she could understand personally. But if the Grand Canyon was more than a third the length of a distance she could barely imagine, it was safe to say she was bedazzled.

When we were still at the KOA in Flagstaff, I wore the ring when I took a short walk through the bit of forest just west of the campground. We could've gone farther, but I just wanted to stretch my legs, so we only wandered for about half an hour. What she liked best about it was the smell of the pines and the forest floor.

I wore the ring and walked the park once or twice, so she could get an idea of our surroundings, and of how different life was here and now.

"Are those ... castles," she started, catching on quickly, "like ours on the inside?"

"The ones that look like mine on the outside," I said, making the distinction carefully, "look a lot like mine on the inside, too. The others are similar – some bigger, some smaller."

"Those are made of wood?" she asked about the cabins.

"Yes. They are permanent structures. People use them for a few days and then leave, and someone else moves in."

"They do no work for living here? You do no work in this place for living here."

"We pay to live here. We do other work to earn the money we pay with."

"Curious," she said. And then, "Ours is not a 'permanent structure'?"

"It doesn't come apart, but we can take it to another place. We'll probably do that soon."

"Why?" I had the feeling when she asked that she was trying to compare my moving the fifth-wheel to a king's traveling the country-side to visit various nobles under his aegis.

"Well, my lady," I said, and launched into as short a lecture as I could manage about the way we – some of us – live now, traveling to visit various places without the perks of nobility. Paying our own way, but taking our time, seeing what interested us, meeting people along the way ....

"Are these ... pilgrimages?"

Who knew that the people of Shropshire undertook pilgrimages? Later, I googled to see what Lady Cecelya might have known about that. Turns out that her home territory, the Welsh Marches, held many routes of pilgrimage.

"Something like that. But not always to religious shrines. To places of personal significance, with stops on the way that turn out to be more interesting than we thought."

"Where are we going next?" she asked.

"I'm not sure," I said. "But before we go anywhere, we need to get a few things clear."

I don't think she appreciated my taking the ring off before I continued. I know she didn't like the clarifications I made when I set the ring back down near the box.

"First," I said, "this is my castle, not yours. All you can claim is the ring and the box, and the lock of hair, whatever good that is to you. This place is mine. Understood?"

There was a long pause before the ring pulsed twice.

"Second, although I respect you as an ancestor, and I'm glad to have met you, I want to help you move on to whatever afterlife you believe in. You don't belong on this plane anymore."

This time her response was the long light that meant "maybe."

"It's not a discussion, my lady," I said. "It is the reality, and I will do everything I can to help you make the transition peacefully."

If I had been wearing the ring when I said that, she'd have understood what I didn't add: that she *would* be transitioning to the next life, whether peacefully or not.

SEVEN

I didn't wear the ring at all for a few days after that.

As I put it on again, I said, "I'll take this off if you start to argue about the terms of our relationship." The double-blink for "yes" and the "fine" she spoke into my mind came at the same time.

Only very simple thoughts were easy to communicate directly. Without writing anything down, she could ask questions like, "What's that," or "What does that mean?" but for long answers, we still needed to write. It helped both of us concentrate. And now she urged me to sit down with our notebook.

"I have remembered more ... details of my life," she said.

"And you want to tell me?" I didn't bother writing that down.

"I have remembered how I died."

"I'm listening," I said, and adjusted the pencil in my hand. I suppose I could sit at the keyboard – I can type faster than I can write longhand, and it would certainly be easier to read, but somehow, it just didn't seem right.

I'm sure there are people who channel spirits through automatic typing, and maybe I would too, if it was a different spirit. But when I wrote by hand, her ring was touching the pen or pencil, and that seemed to help. This time I decided to use a pencil, so it'd be easier to correct the mistakes that were inevitable when she had a lot to say.

"I was thirty-eight years old."

I nodded. I knew that.

"I was at home. I took ill. Our doctors were the best, but our medicine wasn't as advanced as it is today." She had been paying attention. She watched television with me. She gleaned a lot from the books and newspapers I read, too.

"Disease, then?"

"So they allowed themselves to believe," she said. "So I believed, at the time. But now, I wonder. An 'imbalance of humours' covers a lot. Covers *up* a lot." Her English had improved – well, modernized - in the time I'd known her.

"Poison?" Frankly, I could understand why Lady Cecelya might want to do away with her husband, or some of his cronies. She did tend to think of them as traitors to their heritage. But she kept her own opinions to herself, and she produced heirs and ran a profitable home, so why would they want to kill her?

"I think so now," she said, "but not for politics."

I waited a minute or so for her to go on. "Intriguing," I finally said. "For what, then?"

"Oh," she said, "religion."

I will admit that this surprised me. I considered how this might be. His Lordship couldn't have wanted a younger wife that badly, could he? Lady Cecelya was a fine-looking woman, if the ghosty image of herself she sometimes showed me in my mirror was a good indication. Nor was she all that old, even by medieval standards. I waited; she wanted to tell me her story more than she wanted to tease me by withholding it.

"I believe," she said, "that the bishop all but commanded my husband to kill me."

"Because you refused his advances?" Bishops in those days weren't any better at self-control than some of them and some of their priests are now.

"No," she said. I noticed my handwriting getting smaller as it felt like she was lowering her voice. "Because he discovered my secret. My Catholicism was a lie."

By this time, my conversations with Lady Cecelya were like getting lost in a good book. My eyes were focused on writing down what she was conveying to me, and I was usually bent close enough to the paper that all else I could see was the table where I sat.

I rarely looked up, so it was easy to imagine that if I did, I'd see Lady Cecelya's chamber, its stone walls covered with tapestry, carpets on the floor, a lavish bed in one corner ....

The campfires at sites near mine became the scent of the fireplace that warmed her room; the occasional dinner smells were not out of place, either. When I wore her ring, she was living my life through me, and when I was channeling her into our notebook, I was living hers.

I couldn't tell you, then or now, whether I heard her voice the way I'd hear yours if we were chatting, but it felt like I did. When I was alone and so intensely focused as I was when I was 'writing her down,' it wasn't – and didn't really need to be – clear whether I was hearing her voice in the room or in my head. But

I could definitely detect the nuances in her voice, and I did my best to indicate them as I took her dictation.

"Your Catholicism was a lie," I repeated.

"I was well versed, and I was observant," she said. I felt as if she was just at the edge of my peripheral vision, there in her room. I wasn't deluded. I knew it was the twenty-first century, that we were in The Castle, my castle, and that I was writing down what a ghost was telling me. But I felt like I could look up and see her room instead of mine.

"But you didn't believe?"

"My true faith was in the Goddess," she all but whispered.

I went from being surprised to being stunned. Goddess? There was no Wicca in the fourteenth and fifteenth centuries, but there was some Goddess-worship, and certainly some witchcraft. It wasn't anything like the Inquisition made it out to be, but there were cunning women and cunning men who knew herbs and husbandry.

"The bishop," she went on without any prompting, and still in a confidential tone, "found out that I was a witch. I was ... not as skilled at disguise as some of my sisters, and I suppose I thought my rank was some protection."

"But no public accusation, no trial, no execution."

"My husband killed me because the bishop told him to," she said. "It was for them, not for me, that there was nothing public about it.

"But," she said, pausing a moment first, either to think about the circumstances or to give me time to transcribe, "I believe that my sisters - my coven," she clarified, using the modern term, "escaped their notice. Perhaps," she went on, the hint of a smile creeping into her tone, "they thought that without me, the sisters would be lost and return to the Church."

"You don't think that happened?"

"I wasn't their leader. I was a novice. It took them a long time to trust me enough to bring me to their meetings."

"But they did trust you? It wasn't them, having second thoughts?"

"No," she said. "I had proved myself to them. My death was a loss, but it wasn't their destruction."

"Proved yourself ... how?" I doubted the medieval stories of atrocities, but I knew that witches in Lady Cecelya's time weren't Wiccan, weren't bound by the Rede.

"Bringing herbs from our gardens," Lady Cecelya explained. "Bringing money, bringing food." She paused, and I could feel her sorting what to say next. "There were people who used their skills to hurt others, but none of the women training me did that.

"Two of them were midwives, one from a village far enough away that we didn't see her often. They were healers."

I didn't like that she could read my mind, but while I was wearing the ring, she mostly could. She didn't always understand what I was thinking about, but this time she did, and her tone was harder when she responded.

"Can't heal if you can't hex? True enough that if you use the wrong dose, you'll kill instead of save, but that's not the same thing. Did we ever wish anyone ill? Of course we did. The King, his officers ... but we had no opportunity to do more than chant and hope. We were never close enough to them to slip a potion into their ale or a bad mushroom into their dinners.

"And the symptoms were well known – they all had their own doctors who'd have known, and innocents would've been accused, and killed. There were assassination attempts, but we didn't make them."

"So, where did your husband get whatever poison he used on you?"

"From the bishop, of course. Can you think the clerics knew nothing of that? They were allowed to heal, and they knew how to deal out death as well."

That was such a chilling truth that I was surprised the furnace didn't kick on.

EIGHT

I wanted to know more.

But I felt that she was exhausted by reliving – re-dying? – that episode in her life. I waited a few days before I brought it up again. "How did the bishop find out what you were doing?"

"I am not entirely sure, but I suspect now that it was one of the cooks. She may have thought I knew too much about herbs. Or she may have thought I suspected her."

"So she told the bishop?"

"I don't know if she went to him directly, but she could have, if she didn't trust the priest. He dined with us occasionally, and she might have been able to speak with him. It's more likely she told the priest, and he passed along her message. He might have embellished it."

"No one else knew?"

"No one else knew," she said, "but my daughter Margaret may have suspected something. She met me one night when I was returning from a meeting. I told her I heard something outside and went to check."

"She believed you? I'm not sure I would have," I added.

"She chose to believe me, I think. Margaret was very intelligent. She was also quiet, and I don't doubt that she heard more than she was meant to. Sometimes she knew things intuitively that most girls her age didn't know. She was about fifteen when I died."

"If she knew, would she have said anything?"

"I am not sure, but I think not. If she had, I believe she'd have been removed from the house immediately, to avoid any corruption to my wicked ways. Off to a nunnery, where she could've been told what to say against me. So no, I am sure it wasn't Margaret."

Lady Cecelya seemed calmer now, able to talk about it with less distress. I expected she'd been mulling over her memories, trying to come to terms with what had happened to her. And with what she'd done.

I knew that denying the teachings of the Church - apostasy - was a mortal sin. Knowing a few people who had come to Wicca from Catholicism, I also knew that to *feel* it as a sin, you had to still have Catholicism in your heart. If you were truly a convert, guilt would be nothing more than a habit, and eventually you'd break it.

It didn't usually take six hundred years to come fully to a new faith. So I wondered what inspired Lady Cecelya to turn to the witchcraft of her day, and why she still felt so very Catholic.

Of course, when you've been taught something since birth, and when the teaching has been intense, and when alternatives haven't been known to you until your adulthood, it's hard to make more than an intellectual transition to a new belief. And in Lady Cecelya's time, witches were vilified, so joining them wouldn't have been a temptation for very many people of Cecelya's station.

"What made you – "

"Turn to witchcraft?" There was that mind-reading again. At least it saved me the awkwardness of putting my question fully into words. "I was out riding one day," the ghost went on. "I was daydreaming, so when my horse – oh, Suntaria was a fine mare – and when she stumbled, I fell.

"She recovered, and nosed me, but I had twisted my ankle, and couldn't stand right away. Suntaria wandered off a few feet to wait for me, and I sat on the ground and watched my ankle swell.

"I was very annoyed with myself, and trying to get up, but I really couldn't put any weight on my ankle. I hopped to a fallen log and sat down and wondered what on earth I would do next.

"And then," she said, warming to her story-telling, "an old woman appeared. I hadn't seen her coming, but she'd been collecting twigs and mushrooms; her basket was almost full. She asked if I needed help, and when she spoke, I was so startled I almost fell off the log!"

"And she helped you?"

"She did. She pulled some herbs from a pouch around her neck, and spit in them to make a paste, and wrapped them in a rag, and tied it around my ankle.

"Being a high and mighty lady, of course, I was horrified and disgusted, but I couldn't really fight her off – and then she muttered some words over the poultice, and my ankle stopped hurting.

"She knew it, too – probably by the expression on my face rather than by any sorcery." Lady Cecelya laughed. I grinned, but I didn't interrupt. "She told me what the herbs were, and why they were working, but I don't remember now what she said. What I remember is that, old as she looked, her hands and her voice were gentle."

Lady Cecelya was quiet for a few seconds. "She was the first witch you met," I said.

"Yes. We waited a few more minutes, and I was able to stand again. When I told her my horse had stumbled on her right front leg, she felt Suntaria's pastern and her fetlock, and told me the horse was fine, and as soon as I could walk and remount, I'd be fine too.

"She helped me stand, and as I tested my ankle to see if I could at least limp over to Suntaria, she told me that if I wanted to learn more about herbs and the words to say with them, she could teach me."

"She could've brought the horse to you and helped you remount," I pointed out.

"She said she wanted to be sure I could walk. And I told her I thought I would like to learn about the herbs she used. They weren't cooking herbs, and the words, well ... I didn't know how important the words were to the effect, but I wanted to learn them, too."

"And it didn't occur to you that this was sinful?"

"No," she said softly. "Cooks use herbs, doctors use herbs, and sometimes they say words over them. I've heard Cook say 'Now, you just bubble nicely for a few more minutes, and then I'll put you in the bowls,' and I've heard doctors say things in Latin as they administer. So no, I didn't think I was doing anything wrong."

"When did you realize you were studying witchcraft?"

"I rode out – I loved to ride – and met her in the woods a few more times. One day she had two other women with her, one older than she, one younger. I didn't know either of them, but they were nice. We gathered herbs together.

"The next time I saw the first woman again – her name was Malkyn – she asked if I would like to join them to collect herbs by moonlight. She told me when, and I went along. The other two women were with her again, and three more."

"How," I couldn't help asking, "did you get away at night without anyone wondering where you were going?"

"Easily enough," she said, irony thick in her tone. "I said I wanted to pray."

And that lie, I thought, compounded her sin. But she wasn't done with her story, and I wanted to hear the rest, so I didn't state the obvious.

"We did collect herbs. The moon was full enough to see well, but we knew the plants by their scent. I remember datura – for the flying ointment, and invisibility, Malkyn said, but she laughed so I could think she was joking. There were others, but I've forgotten them now.

"Even then I didn't know – didn't let myself know – that they were witches. As the moon rose higher, we wandered deeper into the woods. Suddenly we were in a small clearing, one marked at the edges with stones. Even in moonlight I could see that they were colored, and arranged in certain patterns.

"They sat me down on a flat stone, and Malkyn told me to wait, that she'd take me home when they were done. I had no idea what she was talking about, but I trusted her, so I sat, and watched.

"They stood in a circle. They raised their arms. They chanted together. As one, they went to certain places at the edge of the clearing, including the spot where I was sitting. They didn't speak to me, though, or pull me up into their midst. It was as if I weren't even there.

"*That's* when I realized they must be witches. It was hard to believe, though, because ... there were no men, no devils, no fierce animals. They lit a small fire, but they burned nothing other than wood and a few of the fragrant herbs we'd collected.

"One of them had a cup, and a flagon of ale, and they shared this, and poured a little into the fire to make it hiss and spark, and at that they laughed. They weren't wicked laughs, just delighted ones, as if ... as if they were young women being courted.

"There was more chanting, more stopping at the bigger rocks around the edge of the clearing, and then they all sat down with their hands on the ground. They sat like that for a few minutes, and then Malkyn came back to me and told me it was time for me to go home.

"They walked with me back to where Suntaria was tethered, and ... and I went back. I had been gone some time, but no one at home was alarmed. I slept well that night, and the next day, no one questioned me."

"That wasn't the only time," I suggested.

"No. There were other gatherings, other ... rituals, I learned to call them. And conversations. When we talked, I told them secrets that no one else living had heard, or ever would in that lifetime. I wept, and they comforted me, and I felt ...."

She let her voice, if it was a voice, trail off. I knew she didn't expect me to finish her thought, and I couldn't have if I'd wanted to. I let her take her time.

"I felt understood," she said at last. "I felt that I belonged with them. I felt the way I was supposed to feel in Church."

"And you met with them how long?"

"Since I was twenty-two," she said.

"Sixteen years. That's a long time to keep such a dangerous secret."

"It was not easy," she acknowledged. "If I had not had to go to chapel so often, not had to hear Mass and take communion, I would never have been afraid. But hearing so many times a week that everything I had done was a mortal sin, having to ... make all the motions of agreement, it wore me down.

"I feared for my soul, but I couldn't stop meeting my sisters in the woods. When I died, I was thinking of them. Not of God, not of my husband, not of my children, but of my sisters, the witches.

"And I'm sorry for all of it now, but I am still not sure my contrition is sincere."

NINE

Remembering that, telling me about it, changed her.

I wanted to tell her that witchcraft had survived, had grown, had changed, and that some forms of it were recognized, now, as legitimate religions. I wanted to tell her that the Church was changing, too, but I doubted that she'd be receptive to that.

I wasn't sure how to let her know that I was Wiccan. I'm a retired priestess, and my days of being eager to explain all the tenets of our beliefs are over. But Beltane was almost upon us, and I don't let Sabbats go by without celebrating, so ....

A proper Maypole dance requires more than once dancer; eight is optimum, and there has to be an even number. And a pole. And space. It's not all that practical to set it up at a KOA. But there are other ways to celebrate.

One tradition is to wash your face in Beltane-morning dew, and now that I'm on my own most of the time, that's what I do. It means getting up early, but that's okay. I can always go back to bed after, if I want to.

Morning dew isn't always abundant, but I can usually find a drop or two. I didn't wear the ring when I went out that morning, but when I got back to The Castle, Lady Cecelya wanted to know where I'd been at that hour. I'm pretty sure she had her suspicions.

"Out to wash my face in the morning dew," I said.

"You didn't take me with you."

"You don't have a face."

"I would have enjoyed it."

"I wanted privacy," I said.

"You don't trust me. And you said you wanted to get rid of me." That was about as much as she could communicate without the help of the ring and our notebook.

I put a kettle on for tea. It seemed like a good morning for tea.

"Put on the ring."

"Not right now," I said.

"Are you trying to kill me again?"

"That's a stretch," I said.

"What does that mean?"

"It means that it's not reasonable to think that my not wanting to put the ring on right now means I'm trying to kill you. You have to stretch to reach from what I said to the conclusion you drew." I didn't mention that I could hardly kill her when she was already long dead.

The silence was loud, and it was a few more minutes before the tea-kettle filled it with its warble.

●

Was Lady Cecelya's miff over not being taken out for Beltane-morning dew superficial, I wondered, or was there some reason she'd have liked to be there? Did that condensation have some power beyond the folklore?

I didn't believe that the dew on my face would make me beautiful for the next year, or that walking in it barefoot would cure sore feet. I did those things out of respect for the old ways from which modern Wicca developed, and in memory of the witches who suffered for their trust in the power of Nature.

But back in the day, back in Lady Cecelya's day, people believed that a plant's curative properties could come through the dew on its leaves. In Celtic lands, even including England, they also believed that May Day, the beginning of Summer on the old calendar (and on today's Wiccan calendar), was a time when Nature's powers were enhanced.

Did Cecelya think that something about the Beltane dew could ... bind her more firmly to this plane? Keep her from moving on? Somehow give her more control over my body?

•

I went out again, this time to the Kamp Kitchen, where I got bacon. I don't buy it at the store to cook for myself, but I love it, and that the Kamp Kitchen serves it for breakfast is one reason I like the KOA in Flagstaff. But I brought more than bacon back to The Castle.

"My lady," I said, "I've brought you something."

Her mist manifested over the kitchen island, where I'd set the plate of bacon.

"Not the bacon," she said.

"No, that's for me. But I brought a bit of dew for you. On the handkerchief." I set that down on the island, too. It was really a tissue, artistically (I thought) gathered up, with a moist spot on top where I'd soaked up a bit of the last dew to be found in the shade.

I brought the ring from the box and laid it, stone down, on the dampness.

The mist dissipated and reformed, enveloping the ring.

"Are you enjoying that?"

The mist pulsed twice.

"Are you getting more than enjoyment from it?" I asked.

The mist brightened into a "maybe."

"What else?" It wasn't a yes-or-no question, so there was no answer. "Should I put the ring on and get the notebook?"

"No!" The pulse was brighter than I'd ever seen it before.

"Is there ... magic in it?"

I got another "maybe," but I took it for a yes.

"I'd like you to tell me what magic there is in it," I said. "I study it too, you know."

"Yes."

"So, later?"

There was a pause, and I anticipated a "maybe," but after a few seconds, she her mist pulsed twice for "yes." That made me feel a little better. Maybe.

•

Like any householder, I have chores, so I did some. To work off the nervous energy I found I had, I refolded some clothes. The hamper was empty, the dishes were done, and I didn't have any work projects pending. The light outside was unremarkable, so there were no compelling photo opportunities. The 'fridge was stocked, and I'd picked up mail yesterday. I tried reading, but I couldn't focus.

Around noon, I'd braid a few ribbons, and then wind the braid around a wand. That was the closest I could come to a Maypole without any other dancers.

When it got dark, I'd light my campsite's fire and hop over it, in acknowledgement of Beltane's fertility aspect. At this point, I was more interested in the broader interpretation – creativity in general – but I like keeping that tradition. It has the added advantage of not alarming any of my neighbors.

"My lady, are you ready?" The ring was still in the dew-dampened tissue, but it was dry now.

The mist formed and pulsed "yes."

I put the ring on slowly, and left it at the second knuckle. That made it a little harder to write, but I had the feeling I might need to get it off quickly, and if it wasn't snug, that would be easier. If Lady Cecelya noticed, she didn't say anything.

"You were going to tell me about the magic in the Beltane morning dew," I reminded her. I jotted down the question, along with the date of this conversation.

"At this time of year," she said, "all the plants are growing, so they all have that power to share."

"Okay," I said. That didn't sound ominous, so why was I feeling doomy?

"At Calan Gaeaf," she said, using the Welsh name for the Sabbat I call Samhain, which in this country is generally pronounced saw-wun, "we can use the dew to raise spirits."

That would explain my feeling of foreboding.

"It's not Sa – Calen Gaeaf," I said, almost certainly mangling the pronunciation. It's Calan Mai." I was glad I was at least that familiar with the Welsh names for the Sabbats. And we don't have enough dew to save."

"I don't want to wait – and I may not need more."

"To do what?" I asked, thinking I already knew.

"I don't like being dead," she said. "I don't want to go to Anwnn, what you call the Summerland."

"Being dead in Anwnn isn't like being dead here," I said. "It's like being alive, just somewhere else."

"I don't want to be somewhere else," she insisted.

"You do understand you're not in England, or Wales, don't you? You're not in Shropshire now."

"That's obvious," she said.

I took a deep breath. "You can't ... you can't be not dead on this plane without a body." I was going to add that in Anwnn, she wouldn't need a body, but she interrupted.

"I already use yours sometimes."

"Not the way you used your own, not with volition and control," I said.

"You could –"

"I could," I said, "but I won't. My lady, you are dead these six hundred years. I'm sorry you died young. I'm sorry for all the years you missed, and I'm sorry your death was such a betrayal. But you're not going to live again through me."

I slipped the ring off my finger, glad I'd left it loose. I kept touching it lightly with my left hand, though, so she could still communicate.

"I am stronger now," she offered. It might have been an ordinary comment, but she might have been making a threat.

"Because of the dew," I proposed.

"Yes. I think it could work."

"There isn't any more," I said. "And if there is, it's probably been ... corrupted by now."

"Corrupted?"

"Well, people are out walking around, walking their dogs, and there are animals in the forest, and so even if it wasn't all burned off in the sun by now, it wouldn't be very clean."

"Then we'll have to wait a year," she said, so cheerfully that I knew she did not understand that I was not going to cooperate in her plan to use my body for her come-back.

"My lady, I think you misapprehend," I said. "I'm not going to help you make a new life here in this world. All I am willing to help you do is move on to Anwnn." Or Heaven, I didn't add, because I wasn't sure that's where she thought she'd go.

I could feel her disconnect from the ring, so I got up and put the ring back in its box. I thought about closing the box, and decided against it. When I turned around, the mist, gathered over the once-dewy tissue, was dark, like a monsoon thunderhead. Before I could say anything to her, though, it was gone.

TEN

Knowing a ghost has it in for you is not a good feeling.

This particular ghost might well be addled by her six-hundred-year imprisonment, accidental though it apparently was. And she was feeling powerful, entitled, and thwarted.

I can't say I'm always prepared to fend off a psychic attack. Generally speaking, I don't take the idea very seriously. The way I look at it is that attacking somebody else magically is throwing a tantrum, and people who think to solve problems by throwing tantrums can't very often get their energy much past their own auras.

Given the psychic nature of my relationship with Lady Cecelya, though, I took her potential threat at face value. I put magical protections in place for myself – and on The Castle.

I realized as I was working out what protections to use, and how to activate them, that Lady Cecelya had not occupied many places after she left her own manse in Shropshire. There was the maze-box, of course, but the places where it had rested didn't count, because she hadn't been out of the box.

My fifth-wheel and my truck were the only other places she knew. She'd already implied that she considered my castle her castle, and I knew I needed to make my denial of that pretty substantial. These wards needed to stick.

You know what? I never planned or expected to be in a witch war with a ghost. In the first years I studied Wicca, I heard about witch wars – legendary ones involving at least metaphorical Harry Pottery (although this was way earlier, so we couldn't compare it back then), and real ones, which were much more petulant and rumor-driven.

Witches who weren't Wiccan said Wiccans were all fluffy bunnies and white light, too, and although some are, we're not all like that. I'm certainly not. I take my commitment to the Rede – *an ye harm none, do as ye will* – very seriously, but that doesn't mean I vowed to be a doormat. I am still, and fairly frequently, surprised by the need to set certain boundaries, but I'm never afraid to enforce them.

So it was with Lady Cecelya. I was surprised to meet her, surprised that she was an ancestor, and surprised when she seemed to be turning on me. I wasn't all that surprised that somebody in solitary confinement for six hundred years had gone a little wonky, though, and it wasn't any wonder that she was transferring her anger to me.

She couldn't take revenge on those who had wronged her – not from here, anyway, and assuming her explanation of her death was true. But she was predictably determined to take revenge for what had happened. She seemed to think I owed her something, being a descendant, and, like uncountable others, ancestral and contemporary, she was afraid of death.

Maybe her Catholicism was a lie, but it was also an influence. She said she didn't want to move on to Anwnn, but it sounded to me like the fear of God, of meeting God and enduring whatever punishment might be in store for her, was still with her. Never mind that her Pagan schooling might have suggested a different sort of afterlife. She was afraid to move on.

I have no idea – none of us do, really – what fourteenth century witches thought awaited them after death. Celtic culture wasn't monolithic, it was regional, and by regions, I mean corners of counties. So what Anwnn meant to her I couldn't be sure.

Wicca's understanding of the Summerland is, generally, that we're renewed after death, to our prime, and we have a chance to enjoy an endless summer; hence the name. (Those of us who live in summer-most-of-the-year states hope that "summer" is a subjective term, meaning "ideal" rather than over a hundred degrees all the time.)

We also take it for an opportunity to review and learn from the life we've just left, not facing punishment but learning from our mistakes. That way, when we come back – most of us believe in reincarnation, though we define it rather vaguely – we can address our issues and keep leading better lives.

My Tradition of Wicca holds that we don't "come back until we get it right," but we "come back until we get it all." We come back again and again because it's impossible to "get it all." Every life contributes to the all, so the collective experience isn't finite. My Trad teaches that there's no place else to go but back and forth between life and death – between matter and energy, if you want to reconcile our religion with science.

I'm not saying I want to die. I don't! I'm having a good time here, and I want to keep going as long as I can. And I can't deny that there are a lot of scary *ways* to die. But I'm not afraid of being dead, or of the afterlife. Lady Cecelya was, I think – even though she had proof positive that death isn't an end.

Psych and philosophy aside, I was stuck with an angry ghost, one whose intent seemed to be to live in my body whether I wanted to share or not. I wondered what her teacher – was Malkyn a priestess, or was that too strong a word? – would think about her plan.

I wasn't sure how well it would go over to ask Lady Cecelya to think about that. She might not conclude in my favor! At least up until the nineteenth century, pre-Wicca witches had felt justified in using curses and more material means to defeat their oppressors, religious and political. Malkyn and Lady Cecelya may not have been able to attack kings – or even bishops – but *I* was well within reach.

Being a retired priestess myself, I didn't have all the herbs and tools I once did, when I lived in what the RV community calls a stick-and-brick, a land-bound house. If this had happened a few years ago, I'd have had a veritable apothecary to choose from, close to two hundred reference books, and a full array of altar gear and tools.

Now I had the bare minimum: cooking herbs and what tools and other gear I could fit into one of those rectangular zippered plastic boxes that sets of pillow cases come in. What books I have now are on my e-reader. The coven I once led, and others I'd belonged to, were either disbanded or long-disbanded. Just like Lady Cecelya, I was on my own.

That was fine. I had salt and rosemary. I picked a couple of purple flowers I didn't recognize, and waved my wand over them as I told them to be amethyst, which is a protective gem.

In most magical systems, similarities in one respect – in this case, color – can be taken for similarities in other respects.

Salt represents Earth. I used a bit of incense for Air. I sprinkled in a little bit of cinnamon for Fire, and water for Water. For the fifth element, Spirit, I intoned a charge-blessing.

"By all the Elements, and with the Gods' blessing, I charge this concoction for malice finessing. May He the Horned and She the Three keep me and my Castle safe – so mote it be."

It wasn't eloquent or poetic, but it wasn't meant to be inspirational, either. It was meant to be clear and practical. I stirred the mixture together and put little dabs of it in every corner, at the five centers of every opening (top, bottom, sides, and main plane), and put what was left over in a little cloth pouch I could wear around my neck.

Finally, I put uncooked rice into a shallow bowl and set Lady Cecelya's box in it. That's not a particularly magical thing to do, but you know what they say: rice binds.

I left the secret drawer open, with the ring and her hair in it. "Now, my lady," I whispered as I nestled the box into the white grains, "you are bound to your box, and not to me. You can do me no deceit or harm; as I will, so mote it be."

There was no mist, not that I could see. The Castle didn't feel weird; I didn't feel weird. I trusted the magic. I just wasn't sure Lady Cecelya was aware of it yet. And that made me wonder where she was, and what she was up to.

ELEVEN

Lady Cecelya had never been outside The Castle, not without me.

If she had, somehow, wandered outside on her own, she wouldn't be able to get back in, and I imagined she knew that.

Ghosts don't sleep, and I couldn't imagine that after some of the things she'd said, she wouldn't know that my protection spells were against her machinations. So why wasn't she responding?

I felt the mist gathering, and looked around. It was milky-white on the stairs, a vague outline against the bedroom door. I reached for the box and touched Lady Cecelya's ring.

"Your magic works both ways," she said. "Everything purple will protect me, too. Especially," she added, and I could feel a sneer in her imaginary voice, "your amethyst ring."

Damn. My grandmother's amethyst ring. I wore it frequently, though I wasn't wearing it today. If I had been, it would have been on my side, so to speak. But now, apparently, I couldn't wear it, not while Lady Cecelya was around. Come to think of it, I had a lot of purple in my wardrobe.

I was seriously annoyed with myself for not realizing that the protection spell I'd just done wouldn't pre-empt her using

Grammie's ring. I wasn't really sure why it didn't, but I should have at least considered the possibility.

A ghost's version of *bwahaahaa* is an unpleasant thing to have ricocheting around in your mind.

My protection spell covered deceit, so she couldn't be bluffing – unless she'd come up with this plan before the spell was firmly in place. Could that be a loophole? Maybe. There was enough connection between us already that maybe our magics merged, too – so that even though I'm Wiccan, the magic I do that concerns her can work a little bit by her rules as well as mine.

I pulled my hand away from Lady Cecelya's ring and checked to be sure I wasn't wearing anything purple today before I let myself think about what to do next. The mist shimmered in what passed for my hallway, as if Lady Cecelya were adjusting her skirts.

It would be a simple – and effective, I was sure – thing to put all my purple jewelry into a bowl of salt, covering it completely, and storing it outside The Castle. As for the clothing, well, a visit to the big thrift shop in Flagstaff might be in order.

I could store my purple shirts and sweaters in a box, in the bed of the truck or under The Castle, and get myself some not-purple things as temporary replacements. Those things I could donate back when it was safe to wear my purple clothes again.

But now that it was "on," as they say, how was I going to deal with Lady Cecelya herself? Could I outsmart her? If I put a ring of salt around The Castle, and went somewhere else to plan my strategy, she couldn't follow me ....

But she already couldn't follow me if I didn't have her ring on or with me, and what good would that do anyway? The minute I came back inside, my mind would be vulnerable to her reading it - or so I had to assume. On the other hand, if I stayed here and let her guess at my thoughts, her reaction might give me some idea about defeating her.

I'm not any kind of engineer, so figuring out some physical ghost-trap wasn't going to work. It was a nice idea, though. Something like a glorified domino show, only instead of some intricate pattern of knocked-over dominos, it would culminate in trapping Lady Cecelya back in the maze box. That would've been great.

Except, of course, at the same time I was afraid and angry about her plan to ... possess me, I guess, is the right word, I felt sorry for her. I mean, I'd be cranky if I'd been cooped up in a small box for hundreds of years, only to find out I was supposed to be dead, and then remembered I was killed by my husband at the order of a bishop. Medieval times weren't fun times, and I could see how she'd want a second chance to live out her days.

To live, that is, as a privileged mistress of a large household, with enough social standing to boss quite a number of people around. Worse than the bourgeoisie that I personally wasn't very fond of.

Oh, it may look like I'm living high off the hog - a term Lady Cecelya would definitely understand - because I have a new fifth-wheel trailer. But it's my only home. I don't have any spare mansions laying around to run back to if things go wrong or I get tired of my semi-nomadic lifestyle. And I darn sure don't have any servants. I'm not rich or upper class. I've just adjusted the expense of my life to fit my fairly low income.

So. Yes, I understood why Lady Cecelya might have gone a little bonkers, or even become wholly sociopathic, if not psychopathic, and that was, indeed, too bad. Unfair. But that didn't make it my responsibility to give let her use the rest of my years flouncing around trying to lord it over – okay, *lady* it over – everybody else as if she were still in her manse in Shropshire.

It is my sincere belief that there's no punishment for wrong-doing in the afterlife – unless, of course, you consider realizing what you've done wrong and feeling bad about it to be a punishment. But recognizing our mistakes is how we avoid making them again, and if we don't make up for them in one life, we'll have the chance to make up for them in another.

Not everybody, not even every witch, believes that. I don't think Lady Cecelya believed it, either. Was that because she was raised Catholic and only in later life began to explore a different set of beliefs? Or was it because the Gods she knew through witchcraft were like the one she knew as a Catholic?

I have no idea. I'm not an historian, and I was never Catholic, so I'm not comfortable speculating too much. For some of the currently living witches I know, though, it's a little of both, but most of them are like me: not eager for death, but not afraid of the afterlife, either.

Lady Cecelya seemed unlikely to be convinced that she'd be alright moving on to whatever afterlife she actually believed in, so I wasn't going to try to convince her. But I couldn't help wondering whether there was more to her reluctance than wanting a chance at the twenty-or-more years she'd have had if her husband hadn't obeyed his bishop.

Had she done something herself that would've counted against her before any of the gods she knew about? I doubted that asking her would get me very far, and there was nothing online about her being any kind of wicked woman.

I don't read many ghost stories, but I do read a lot of mysteries. Here I had one in real life, so to speak, about Cecelya deHulle's past. My trying to solve it might buy my lady a little more time on this plane. Once I figured it out and addressed it with her, though, she was outta here.

TWELVE

When I went online to research Lady Cecelya's family, I revisited my own connections to the line.

I traced Lady Cecelya's family back to Guy Collefey, who died around 1105. My own line was through Lady Cecelya's mother, Aline Walensis, whose line allegedly went back to the Welsh gods. I wondered if that meant I out-ranked Lady Cecelya, but I decided not to broach that subject.

I wasn't looking for royalty, either. The nobility had died out of all of my lines by the time I was born, and she was herself of noble blood. What I wanted to know was whether that noble blood hid any secrets that might be frightening Lady Cecelya not *to* death, but *from* death.

You know how the family line websites are: they give you names and dates, which are usually in the ballpark, but any details and stories are posted by descendants who've heard them, and that's all one long game of *Telephone*. And not everybody who has a family story posts it.

If you're lucky, some of the people you find on the genealogy pages were of high enough rank – like Lady Cecelya – to be noted historically. In those cases, there were sometimes anecdotes noted by their contemporaries, and handed down relatively (no pun intended) unchanged.

They needed to be teased out of various histories, like delicate bones out of a dinosaur dig, but sometimes, you came across something intriguing, or even useful. After a few days of intense digging through bits of nineteenth- and early twentieth-century books that were available online, I found a couple of things that got me thinking.

First, a couple of names occurred more than once. Some women outlived their first husbands and married again – and one or two of them, in Lady Cecelya's and my converging lines, married relatives of their first husbands. This left women like Lady Cecelya with older men who were both uncles and cousins. One or two lines in dry old books suggested that Lady Cecelya had been bedded by a much older man who was at least her grand-uncle.

There were also rumors about Lady Cecelya preparing for a trip abroad, which was then canceled. Had her mother's uncle impregnated her? Was she to be sent away to have the baby? Did something happen, so that she didn't need to go?

A good Catholic girl, still was in her teens, she'd have felt guilty for her own rape, especially if she cooperated under threat. And if she'd lost the baby, she'd have felt guilty about that, too. Especially if she'd lost the baby accidentally on purpose.

I had no doubt that this sort of thing happened, and not infrequently. Abortifacients were well-known then, and what with marriages and other unions not always being for love, the need for them was not unknown, either.

If Lady Cecelya had aborted a baby – well, in her time it *might* not have been a mortal sin.

The idea was that an abortion wasn't murder if it occurred before ensoulment, and a fetus wasn't deemed to have a soul before it quickened. What that meant was that an abortion before the fourth month of a pregnancy wasn't murder.

But ... a girl might not realize she was pregnant before she felt the child move inside her – and once she felt it move, an abortion was murder.

If any of these rumors were true, if Lady Cecelya had aborted a pregnancy after ensoulment, she'd committed a mortal sin. Later, she'd commit another: apostasy, when she began to embrace witchcraft and reject her Catholic beliefs. But as a woman, childless though I am, I could see that she'd take the abortion more to heart than the apostasy.

About this, I thought, I needed to ask.

These days, I didn't wear her ring any more. I held it in my hand, connecting us without risk of it getting stuck on my finger. Picking it up the next morning, I called out to see if Lady Cecelya would "talk" to me.

My lady? I need to ask you something."

The mist coalesced over the kitchen island, looking like a sooty basketball-sized sphere. She was evidently not in a good mood.

"I've been doing some research," I said. "About our families."

The mist wiggled a little.

"I'm wondering if something happened between you and one of your maternal grand-uncles."

The mist condensed until it was the size of tennis ball, and then it sort of exploded, disappearing completely.

"I'll take that for a yes," I said, staying calm. For over six hundred years she'd had to keep that secret, and I had triggered a reliving of what was probably the biggest trauma of her life. "I can only guess how it made you feel," I said.

I heard screaming in my mind.

"It wasn't your fault," I said, aloud and in writing.

Over the course of two or three minutes, the screaming subsided, and I heard – and felt – sobbing instead.

"It wasn't your fault," I repeated. "It was something that happened to you, not something you did wrong. And even the baby," I whispered after a moment. If I could have hugged her, I would have. Instead, I held the ring between my hands.

"I murdered it," she gasped.

"Your life could have been in danger. You didn't have many choices. He couldn't marry you. That wasn't your fault."

"It's a mortal sin. I never confessed," she said.

There was nothing I could say. The depth of her grief and fear – and anger, I could feel anger, too – was beyond anything in my personal experience.

After another minute or so, she said, "It wouldn't have been a legitimate confession. I didn't truly repent ridding myself of that monster's spawn." She finished that thought, and then fell back into her sorrow. "But the baby was innocent ... and I was not."

My surprise was unarticulated, but she understood it.

"No, I was a virgin," she told me. "Innocent in that respect, at least." I guessed the following pause was filled with her recollection of other, not so innocent encounters. "But not innocent of murder," she said. Now her voice felt husky. Her grief was, for the moment, under control, and she felt, for the moment, ready to face the consequences.

"You were apostate later," I said.

"Another mortal sin," she agreed. "But it didn't ... it didn't take the place of ...."

"I understand, Lady Cecelya. But perhaps ... easier to be condemned for that than the other?"

"I wanted it to be," she said. "But it wasn't. I never confessed either offense," she said. "If I had known I was to die, I would have, but ... I am not sure they would have allowed me a priest. The bishop was a cruel man."

"Can you truly repent now, Lady Cecelya?"

"I ... I don't know," she said. "But now that my secrets are not secret anymore, I think I can bear to ask myself that question. Thank you."

"Happy to help," I said. The mist dissipated, slowly, and after a moment I got up and put the ring back in its box. The maze-box was still open, and still in its bowl of rice. That wasn't going to change in the foreseeable future.

From experience with the living, I thought it entirely possible that the thanks Lady Cecelya had just given me would be withdrawn. Self-examination is usually easier promised than undertaken, and, of course, it's not something you can do once and for all. It's a process, and it can be damned uncomfortable – in Lady Cecelya's case, perhaps literally damned.

As a Wiccan, I don't believe in damnation. We can turn away from our Goddess, from what is sacred, but she, being life itself, cannot turn away from us. Even if we can't turn ourselves back toward the Goddess, she – because she is all that is –

continues to embrace us. We may condemn each other or ourselves, but we are never damned by our deity. If that were possible in our thealogy, I can't imagine the terror we'd live with every day.

THIRTEEN

"I never confessed either offense."

So much for her witchcraft. She learned it, she practiced it, but it never replaced her belief in the God of her youth. She'd wanted it to, but either there hadn't been a significantly different theology, or there hadn't been one at all. She still felt the need for Catholic sacraments.

"I never confessed either offense."

I kept hearing her say this. I was always aware of what in audible speech we'd call her tone, always aware of what she was feeling through our conversations. Her distress, her torment, was almost as intense for me as it was for her.

"I never confessed either offense."

There had to be something I could do. I wanted to send her on her way, but not in a state of mortal terror. My belief in the afterlife isn't like hers, and I believe that the mood you're in when you cross over influences your experience on the other side.

I tried reasoning with her. "If you still feel a need to confess your witchcraft," I said, "then you never really rejected Catholicism. So it's a serious sin, but maybe not irredeemable."

"It was a mortal sin," she said. "And I died unconfessed. I will be sent to Hell. I know I deserve it, but I am afraid."

"Then your contrition is sincere," I said. "Surely that counts for something."

"Not if I am unconfessed."

I wanted her to go, but I wanted her to go with a clear conscience. Pretty obviously, this would require the services of a Catholic priest. I thought that in a pinch, an Episcopal cleric might be able to help, but .... I took my laptop outside and started yet another search.

Lady Cecelya didn't need to know anything about my idea until I found out whether it would work or not. There are Catholic churches in Flagstaff, so I started there, with Our Lady of the Peaks.

I have enough formerly Catholic friends to know that speaking to the dead to divine or change the future is forbidden, and has been since the Church was new. But this, though it would involve speaking to the dead, wasn't to divine anything, at least not on the priest's part.

All he needed to do was hear her confession and absolve her of her sins. Providing we could establish some way of his hearing her, and providing she really could repent.

Would that be changing the future? No more than any confession and absolution did, I thought, but I wasn't sure. My own faith's thealogy I understand, but Catholicism? Nope. We definitely needed a priest.

She had already confessed, but to me: to someone who wasn't Catholic and wouldn't be ordained even if she was, was no confession at all. Finding a real priest wouldn't be too hard, but finding one who was willing to take a ghost's confession, that might be tricky.

To my great surprise, the receptionist at Our Lady of the Peaks – that would be the San Francisco Peaks, near Flagstaff – called back the day after I e-mailed the church.

"Father Michael would like you to make an appointment so he can talk with you about your ... situation," she said.

I'd been pretty straightforward about my question, and took it for a good sign that they were willing to talk to me at all. It turned out Father Michael could see me the next day, at 10:30 in the morning. So far, so good, as long as didn't have the men in white coats waiting for me.

●

"So," he said, after we'd said good morning and he'd waved me to a comfortable chair in his office, "you want me to take a ghost's confession. Would you like some coffee?"

"Tea would be great, Father, if you have it; and yes, I need someone to take a ghost's confession."

He didn't bat an eye. He pushed a button on his intercom and asked someone to bring tea, and then he said, "And you're not Catholic yourself."

"No, Father, I'm not."

I know a fair number of non-Catholics who are uncomfortable addressing a priest as "Father." I get that – these men are not our parents; indeed, their title doesn't imply that they are our secular fathers, but that they're standing in for our heavenly father.

My Tradition of Wicca sees our God as a brother and mentor rather than a father, though of course he has father aspects. But it still doesn't bother me to call a priest "Father." I guess that's because my clerical title is Lady, and if I'm going to expect priests and ministers of other faiths to use my title, I have to be fine with using theirs.

It didn't even seem strange to call Lady Cecelya "lady," either, because I'm very aware that in my case, it's a religious designation, and in hers, it's a mark of social rank. To my way of thinking and hearing, those two usages of "lady" are no more confusing than any other homonyms.

However, I wasn't asking Father Michael to call me Lady Seelie. I just wanted him to consider hearing my ghost's confession.

"How do you propose I communicate with this ghost?"

"I'm not sure," I admitted. "I do it by holding her ring, and letting her speak in my mind. Sometimes I write everything down." I waited for him to ask for a psychiatrist's affirmation that I was not, in fact, delusional.

"How did you ... find this ghost?" he asked instead. "Does it haunt your house?"

I shook my head. "She was trapped in an antique maze-box – a puzzle box – that a friend sent to me. When I opened it, I found a ring and a lock of hair. And a few days later, she ... revealed herself to me."

He steepled his fingers and considered this for a moment. "If you have time," he said, "I'd like you to tell me the whole story."

I had time, and I was encouraged by his sounding interested. Did he believe me? I thought he did. Poking around online, I couldn't find anything to indicate that Catholics don't – can't – believe in ghosts. Did Father Michael believe in them theoretically, or from experience? I had no idea. But apparently he had time, too, so I told him the whole story, albeit the short version.

"It doesn't sound like you need an exorcism," he said when I was finished.

I blinked. "It never crossed my mind," I said. "She's not a demon. If she were, I'd find a way to get rid of her myself. She is the ghost of an historical personage. I think she's a little ...." I searched for the word. "I think she's a little unhinged, but who wouldn't be after what she's been through?"

"Six hundred years in solitary confinement, not even knowing she's dead, and then realizing she's five thousand miles from home, and remembering that she was murdered ... and that she died unconfessed," he mused, nodding.

"Do you believe me, Father? Do you believe my story?"

"I won't disbelieve," he said. "I just don't have the experience to put this in context. The only ghosts that old that I know of are ... castle ghosts," he said, half-grinning because I'd told him the name of the my fifth-wheel. "Battlement ghosts," he amended. "Or women in white in graveyards, and I've never seen one myself.

"I did know somebody, once, who saw her sister's ghost now and again, a sister who died in childhood. She thought she might be imagining it, but she wanted to know if it was a sin to see it, either way."

"Was it?"

"I didn't think so, no," he said. "We said some prayers together, and on her birthday – the dead sister's – was the last time the lady saw the ghost. Who knows which of their souls was rested."

"Sounds like both, maybe," I said. Wiccan clergy don't have collars or any other recognizable gear to wear outside of Circle, but we can't always help feeling the role, at least a little, when pastoral duties come into a conversation.

"This is not a personal ghost for you," he said, not expecting me to answer. "It seems to be attached to the ring, or the box ... or both."

"That's what I think," I said. "I've got the box in rice, to bind any energy she might get from it – because as I said, sometimes she takes a pretty aggressive attitude, and makes threats."

"As many do, when they are angry and frightened."

"Exactly." I was sure the priest understood my dilemma. I just wasn't sure whether he could – or would – help me resolve it.

FOURTEEN

"I am inclined," he said, his tone making it clear that he was choosing his words carefully, "to say I can't help you.

Maybe I looked disappointed, because I was. "But to be fair," he went on, I should meet – try to meet – your ghost before I give you a final answer."

I found that encouraging, given that I hadn't expected him – anyone – to listen to my story or take me seriously to begin with.

"Thank you," I said. "You're welcome to come by at your convenience. I appreciate your open-mindedness."

Smiling faintly, he glanced at the weekly calendar on his desk. "Later this afternoon would work for me," he said. "Around three-thirty?"

"That would be just fine," I said. "Thanks again." I'd already told him what space I was in at the KOA. He wouldn't have far to walk from the guest parking area. "You'll need to check in at the office, so I can meet you there."

"Sounds like a plan," he said, and grinned. He stood up and came around his desk to shake my hand and see me out to my car.

Father Michael wasn't tall, but he was slender, and had shoulder-length, not quite carrot-top, hair. I thought he looked a little like a young Shaun White, and wondered if he skied or snow-boarded too. After all, the San Francisco Peaks are nearby, and there are four lifts at Snowbowl. He looked like he did something to stay fit.

•

He was early; I met him when he was coming out of the office after having told the desk clerk he was visiting me. We walked back up to The Castle together.

"Niiice," he said.

"Thanks. Come on in."

Fit though the Father was, I was glad I had the yoga step at the bottom of the stairs. The rise is high, and it's less awkward when it doesn't feel so much like a stair-climber at the gym.

"Even more impressive inside," he said.

"Well, it's home," I said.

"You're really full-timing?"

It was my turn to be impressed. Not many people who didn't live in an RV knew the term. "I am. I'll be on my way to New Mexico in a while, but I'm hoping to get this situation worked out first."

"Of course," he said. "I hope I'll be able to help." There was something odd about his tone, but I couldn't put my finger on it.

"This is the box," I said, gesturing towards it. I wondered if I should explain, more than I already had, why it was sitting in a shallow bed of rice.

"And the rice ... protects it from moisture, being as it's so old?" By the tone of his voice, I understood then that he was being discreet. Apparently he remembered what I'd told him about binding Lady Cecelya.

"Even in Arizona, you can't be too careful," I said. "That's her ring, and a lock of her hair." Then I thought I'd better remember my manners. "Lady Cecelya, we have a visitor," I said, as if she were standing across the room.

"Glad to meet you, my lady," Father Michael said, averting my introduction dilemma. "I'm Michael Carmichael."

We waited, as if standing in silence was an ordinary thing to do. I suppose it is, in some circumstances; for me, this wasn't one of them. I wasn't second-guessing myself about bringing Father Michael here, but I was hoping Lady Cecelya would be curious, if not cooperative.

I was keeping my eyes open for any mist, and a few seconds later, I noticed what looked like fuzzy air over the kitchen island. I glanced over, wanting to alert Father Michael without breaking the silence. He nodded almost imperceptibly and followed my gaze.

His eyes widened, and I knew he'd seen the mist that was Lady Cecelya's typical manifestation. His nostrils flared a little as he took a deep breath and tried to look nonchalant at the same time.

I stepped back toward the couch and picked up her ring, gingerly, between two fingers. I didn't want her to connect with me right now. We needed to know if Father Michael could communicate with her. I opened my other hand to show him what to do. He copied my gesture and I dropped the ring onto his palm.

I closed my fingers over my empty hand as a silent suggestion, but he wasn't watching me; he didn't need to. His fingers closed over Lady Cecelya's ring, not tightly, but enough that he had full contact with it.

He stepped a little closer to the mist. That made it easier for me to look back and forth between Lady Cecelya and Father Michael. I was trying to get some idea of what, if anything, might be passing between them. But for a few seconds, I wasn't sure they had any contact.

"Yes, I am a priest," he said. Then his brow furrowed. "Maybe," he said, obviously answering a question. "I'm not sure it's allowed, but I would like to help you."

He took a really deep breath then, and looked at me. Father to a flock he may have been, but at that moment, he was a gobsmacked young man, wondering whether to believe his own senses.

"She's real," I said.

His expression was disbelieving. I knew how he felt. I couldn't relate to the confusion he was feeling: he was communing with the dead, which is generally frowned upon by the Church. But he wasn't divining, not trying to control the future or seeking to benefit from special knowledge.

He might not have been breaking any rules, but he was definitely intellectually and emotionally surprised to be talking to a ghost in a stranger's fifth-wheel. He shook his head slightly, and I half-smiled and shrugged.

"I think it could work," he said. "But I have to check with my bishop before I can ...." His voice trailed off because he could feel the conversation going wrong. The mist darkened. He looked at his hand and took his fingers off her ring.

I took the ring from him and put it back in Lady Cecelya's maze-box. By the time I turned back, the darkened mist was almost dissipated.

"I'm sorry," I said. "I should have warned you not to – "

"Mention a bishop," he finished with me. "I had thought about that, but I forgot. This whole encounter was amazing, and I stumbled in my duty," he said.

"It's stumble-worthy," I said. "What do you think the regional bishop will say?"

"I think he'll say this is off-limits," Father Michael said. I heard again that strange tone in his voice.

"Buuut?"

"Let's just wait and see what he makes of it," Father Michael said.

"Yes, let's," I said. "Would you like some tea, maybe a snack before you go?" In my experience, food and drink are grounding, and most people – even people who are used to things like this – need to ground after an occult experience. Father Michael wasn't used to it.

FIFTEEN

"That ... that would be nice," he said. "Thank you."

He sat down at the table and let me put the kettle on and rummage in the pantry and 'fridge. "Whatever happens, thank you for this adventure."

"You're welcome ... and thank you, for your willingness to have it. I hope it's not over yet, but I appreciate your coming this far."

"I hope I can go a little farther, but I'm guessing the bishop will think I've gone too far already. Now," he said, "tell me how you came to live full-time in a fifth-wheel."

"Would you like the rest of the tour first? Not that there's a lot more to see."

"Sure," he said, and sounded genuinely interested.

I went up the two stairs to the bedroom ahead of him, and opened the door. "The bedroom. Queen bed, and plenty of closet space for one person. There's a sliding door to the bathroom here," I said, and went through it. He followed.

"Roomier than I'd have thought." I silently thanked him for not making fun of my old teddy bear, which was leaning against the pillows on my bed. He represents a lot that I couldn't keep when I moved into The Castle.

"The shower doors are a little hard to keep clean," I told him. "A lot of owners replace them with a curved shower rod and a curtain, but I'm good with it like this. I like the counter space, too. And this door takes us back into the hall."

"It feels larger than it is," he said, nodding appreciatively.

"That's how I feel about it.

"Is it hard to tow?"

"It can be a little challenging," I said. "And I do try to book pull-through sites so I don't have to back up – I'm not very good at that yet. But it's easy to hook up and unhook. I manage pretty well, and I think it'll get easier."

"This is a nice campground."

"Yes, it is. There's a Kamp Kitchen – I can get bacon in the morning without having to cook it myself."

"Well, then, what else do you need?" His laugh was pleasant. He wasn't old enough to seem very fatherly; to me, he came across as very brotherly. I had the sense that he was content with his calling. "But how did you ... make the decision to live like this?"

"I've worked from home for years," I said, "and over my lunch hour, I started watching little half-hour shows about the RV life. Some of the people featured were looking for a trailer for vacations, and some were looking to sell their houses and go full-time. It intrigued me.

"And then I did the math, and realized I could reduce my weekly – and hence my monthly – costs considerably if I bought an RV big enough to live in."

"And you can travel when you want to."

"I can. I do miss my friends, but I swing back to Tucson, where I used to live, now and again. There are several places I can park there, and see everybody. Flagstaff is kind of my second home base., but between here and there, I make new friends everywhere I go."

"And you can leave people behind when you want to, too."

"Some more easily than others." We chuckled together, and then the tea-kettle made its noise. While the tea was cooling to drinkable, I made some snacks with crackers and cheese and cherry tomatoes. I suppose we must've chatted after that, but I don't remember what about.

●

I heard back from him in a couple of days. Lady Cecelya still hadn't manifested. She knew perfectly well why I'd called the priest, and apparently – Father Michael didn't tell me what she said to him – she'd been okay with the idea of his helping her. Until he'd mentioned his bishop. She wouldn't understand the term, but that "triggered" her.

My theory was that Lady Cecelya was right on the edge of sanity. To me, that seemed like a natural consequence of her perspective. Honestly, I didn't blame her for any of her choices. Life in the Middle Ages, even for the nobility, wasn't easy. Being a woman didn't make it any easier.

Queens and regent mothers, and of course, abbesses, had real power, but women like Lady Cecelya were married young, and it didn't help matters that husbands were not given much choice about their marriages, either. Having servants sometimes meant that noblewomen had more free time, but what they could do with it was limited.

Lady Cecelya enjoyed playing games, and riding – I knew that - but as she came to understand the freedoms I had, even things I considered chores, it began to annoy her.

"Your clothes are a lot easier," she'd said to me, more than once. "Your – truck? – has never thrown you."

When it came up, she'd asked how I learned about witchcraft, and she was stunned to find out I'd first learned of it from a book.

But lately, she resented me, and the limitations I put on her, as much as she did the whole of her previous life. And now I'd brought somebody around who was going to involve another bishop.

Never mind that this bishop couldn't make physical advances to her. From her perspective, he could order another death, and enforce her condemnation to Hell. There wasn't much I could say to reassure her about that, either.

I knew it wouldn't do any good to explain to her that modern witches didn't believe in Hell; I didn't even try. I wasn't looking forward to telling her whatever the bishop had to say, either. I was pretty sure he'd deny the request for Father Michael to hear her confession and absolve her.

Then again, I wasn't entirely sure that she was truly repentant of her sins, at least not of the abortion, and for both her and Father Michael that was going to be critical. Being truly sorry she had no other alternatives wasn't going to be enough. I took advantage of the interlude between Michael's visit and his next call, and just enjoyed my ordinary life.

There's lots to enjoy in the Flagstaff area. There are Native ruins to tour, museums to visit - and brew pubs. Old Flagstaff is fun to walk, and for a couple of days, I went into town and pretended that I didn't live in a haunted castle.

•

When I saw who was calling, I stepped outside before I answered the phone. Lady Cecelya was getting better at making a connection to me even when I wasn't holding her ring, and I didn't want her to overhear whatever Father Michael had to say.

"Hello, Father," I said.

"Hello, Seelie." The politely disapproving look I'd given him the first time he addressed me - automatically, I'm sure, as I *was* consulting him in his clerical capacity - as "my child" had done its job, and he called me by my first name now.

"You've heard from your bishop?"

"I have," he said. "He said it was up to me. But he sounded like he thought I should decline. It's only technically alright. In our conversation, the phrase 'slippery slope' came up."

"But he left it up to you."

"He did." There was that funny tone of voice again.

"Father, why don't you just tell me what's going on."

"Maybe not over the phone," he said.

"And maybe not here, either? Do you want to meet somewhere in town?"

"Can't do it today," he said. "How about tomorrow? Would Flagstaff Brewing be okay? Around noon?"

"Sure." I'd been there yesterday, but I didn't think it was too soon for another order of poutine.

That was about it for that phone call. The next day's conversation was more interesting.

SIXTEEN

I don't know if it's because I'm older than Father Michael ....

Maybe it's because I'm not a Catholic and thus not going to show up at a Mass or talk to anybody who knows him, or because it did come up that I'm an ordained Wiccan priestess. But he seemed comfortable talking to me about some pretty burdensome stuff.

Over my Sasquatch Stout and poutine, and his Bitterroot ESB and grilled pear salad, he told me his story.

"I've never doubted my calling," he said. "I love the Mass, and I love the pastoral work, especially with teenagers. It's the ... the ...." He paused for a moment, covering his search for words with a bite of salad.

"The out-of-date perception of reality," he finally said. "Clinging to interpretations and limitations that no longer serve the Church's purpose.

"Do you think," he said, "that Jesus' gospel was familiar to people when he started preaching? No, of course it wasn't," he said, giving me, maybe, a little taste of his sermon style. "Jesus was a radical because his beliefs were radical, and they were radical because they spoke to the hearts of the people he ministered to, rather than to the needs of the ruling class.

"The Church is beginning to catch up now, and starting to atone for its sins. And some of us – with the nuns taking point, I might add – are ahead of the Vatican's curve. I like to think I am among them. But a lot of us, even knowing the problems the Church faces and knowing – intellectually – that we need to be more sensitive to social changes, get back to leading social change – can't get behind that emotionally."

He paused to wet his whistle, and I, nodding, said, "And your bishop knows what he needs to do, but isn't all that enthusiastic?"

Father Michael nodded. "The question you've brought to us isn't at all representative, and not something he and I can see all that differently. Neither of us knows how to look at it, really, much less how to see it." He paused again, looking to see if I understood.

I thought I did. "There are other issues, though, about which you do disagree – enough to force him out of his comfort zone?"

He grinned, and nodded. "If there were more priests waiting for placement, I'd probably be reassigned already," he said, almost cheerfully. "It's not really like we're at loggerheads, but if we were, we'd be in a stalemate right now."

"I think I get it. So ... what you decide to do about Lady Cecelya is a test? Sort of a test?"

He looked thoughtful. Apparently it wasn't an easy yes-or-no question. "Maybe, but I think 'turning point' might be more accurate. It's not just about his being my diocesan superior and whether I keep my job or not. It's a chance for us to establish new common ground, with both of us having to venture into unknown territory. He wasn't always staid," he added.

"No?" Thereby hung a tale, but I didn't know how much of it I'd get to hear.

"He's in his late sixties now, but in *the* sixties, he was ... a more enthusiastic supporter of Vatican II than his immediate superiors were. I think that may be why he's not an Archbishop, or even a Primate by now. He made some ... career limiting moves back then. And I think he doesn't want to do to anyone else the way he was done to."

I nodded. My faith isn't centralized enough for that sort of thing to happen nationally, much less internationally. But within local and regional groups, there's plenty of personal politics, so I understood him even if I wasn't familiar with the hierarchical details.

"So ... this might be a chance to let everything else go, and advance together?"

"In personal growth, I think so. I hope so. But you have to understand that in leaving it up to me, he's offering to take responsibility for my decision and that's huge."

I nodded again. "But you're not sure what he'd like you to decide?"

Father Michael shook his head. "It's not that. It's not a question of which decision would make him happiest. Certainly declining your request would make for less paperwork for both of us, but ...."

He shook his head, grinned, and then continued more somberly. "It's about, or, I should say, it *feels* like it's about whether I am serious about my minor rebellions, and whether he is still the man he used to be. All in the context of service to the Church.

"Vatican Two was in nineteen sixty-four, but Pope John announced it in nineteen fifty-nine, and just the announcement was enough to ruffle a lot of feathers." He looked at me; I was cocking my head at him. "No," he said, answering my unasked question. "I wasn't even born then, and the bishop was very young, perhaps even precocious in knowing his calling so soon. But I've listened to him, and I've studied that conclave."

I nodded, and we both ate a little more, knowing Father Michael's commentary wasn't finished.

"I guess a lot of people – even Catholics," he went on after a couple of minutes, "think V-Two's main accomplishment was taking the Mass out of Latin and putting it in English – or whatever language people spoke at home – but there was more to it than that.

"It was about bringing the Church back to the people," he said. His passion was quiet, but intense. "We're supposed to be a family, to emphasize not only secular families, but to *be* a family, and not to support the elite. We're supposed to be the ninety-nine per-cent," he said.

"That's always been my understanding. Starting with Jesus," I added.

Father Michael nodded. He was sure enough that I got what he was saying that he took a couple more minutes to address his salad again. I'd been munching my fries the whole time, but I'd been neglecting my beer. We were quite for a little bit. I wanted, but didn't want, to ask him what he thought he'd do.

"I know that Lady Cecelya's more or less part of the one per-cent, but she was at the low end of the nobility scale, and she was certainly taken advantage of, by the social hierarchy and by the Church.

"I think of her as a frightened young girl, first enduring rape, and then realizing she was with child, and being afraid not only of secular and ecclesiastical punishment, but of dying, and of the courage it must've taken for her to ... seek an end to her pregnancy," he said.

He had lowered his voice, and was shaking his head as he spoke. He looked up at me, and said, "She's exactly who the Church is supposed to be helping."

He went back to his salad then, poking at it as much as eating it. We were quiet another little time. With just a few bits of lettuce left on his plate, he put his fork down and picked up his beer. He finished that, set the glass down, and looked me in the eye.

"Seelie," he said, "I'm going to hear Lady Cecelya's confession, and if she's truly repentant ...."

SEVENTEEN

When I got home, I was sure I never needed to eat again.

I went right to the box and picked up Lady Cecelya's ring. "Lady Cecelya, stop pouting and come out. I have news." I didn't usually talk to her like that, because she tended to get sulky if she didn't get the respect she thought she deserved, but I was too pleased to care.

The mist manifested. She was immediately aware that I was holding her ring. "What?"

"The bishop – no, don't flounce away, just listen! The bishop left it up the Father Michael whether or not to hear your confession."

The mist had started out a bit murky, and gotten darker when I mentioned the bishop, but now it lightened, and I felt her presence in my mind more than I saw it over the kitchen island.

"And he's decided that he will!" She was as excited as I hoped she'd be, but not for long. "When?"

"Whenever we want to arrange it," I said. "He said that he holds confession on Tuesday evenings and Saturday mornings. If you want to go to his church ... or he can come here. It's up to you, my lady."

She was quiet, but I could feel her considering this news, and the new decision she had to make.

"You do have to be truly repentant," I reminded her.

"I know," she said. "I am truly sorry for ending an innocent life, when I remember that the baby was innocent of its father's sin. It seems unfair ...."

"You're thinking of Exodus and Deuteronomy," I guessed. Wiccan I am, and the Christian Bible's not my book, but I am familiar with it, and many of the New Testament's teachings are compatible with my beliefs. The Old Testament, not so much, but as I understand Christianity, Jesus made new rules, changed the relationship between God and his people. A lot of it, anyway. And nothing in my faith forbids me from being familiar with other religions.

"Yes," she said.

"We're well past the third and fourth generation," I said. Those Old Testament books talk about their fathers' sins being visited on their children to the third and fourth generations.

Personally, I thought that was in the context of teaching and belief, and not necessarily personal sins like rape: a baby isn't responsible for the way it was conceived. Adults, on the other hand, no matter how they're brought up, can be held responsible for their beliefs and behaviors. As far as I was concerned, those verses were talking about adult children, and in a context of lineage and community.

I wondered if that would make Lady Cecelya feel much better, though. She was taking it all very personally, as her religious schooling had taught her to do. But I was holding her ring, so she had access to my thoughts. She could take them into account or not as she thought about confessing to Father Michael.

There was something else, though. It was as misty to my thought as Lady Cecelya's manifestation was to my eyes. "What else?" I asked.

"If I confess, and he believes that I am contrite, and absolves me, I will have to leave," she said. "Even if I can go to Heaven – surely I have been in Purgatory these last six hundred years, and that's long enough – I will have to leave here. And you."

"Well, yes," I said. "But I think that is only sorrowful now, when you don't know how Heaven will feel. When you are there –"

"I don't want to forget you. You have been kind to me," she said.

"Oh, I don't think you'll forget me. You'll still have all your memories – and if they are not pleasant now, they will be when you see everything through God's love." I had no idea whether that was consistent with Catholic theology, but I thought it ought to be.

"Are you sure?"

"I'm not Catholic," I said, "so no. But you can ask Father Michael. You can ask him about anything that scares you. He's a good man, and he's willing to confess you at some risk to his own position in the Church."

This was news to Lady Cecelya. I felt her surprise. It became clear to me that the idea of a cleric being willing to take a risk of any kind for a parishioner was one that had never occurred to her.

"It was easy to talk to him," she remembered. Clearly she meant more than that she'd been able to communicate through the ring with him as she did with me. "Can I talk to him and then decide about confession?"

"Of course," I told her, hoping I wasn't overstepping by speaking for Father Michael. I wasn't very worried about it, though.

•

Together, we decided that Lady Cecelya would talk to Father Michael in the quiet setting of the woodland next to the KOA. He came back out a day or two later, around mid-morning. I said I'd have lunch ready when they got back, and off he went, with her ring on his pinky finger.

I wasn't going to ask either of them what they talked about. Father Michael wouldn't tell me, because even though she wasn't confessing to him yet, the three of us were in agreement that her conversations with him were private, and privileged.

Lunch was sandwiches, and Father Michael and I ate at about one in the afternoon. We sat outside, in the Adirondack chairs that furnished the patio of my campsite. Assured that we wouldn't be talking about her, Lady Cecelya was happy to have some time to herself. She had a lot to think about.

"I can't believe I've never walked in these woods before," Father Michael said. We talked about Eldon Pueblo, which was a little farther away than their stroll had taken them, but still within walking distance of the KOA.

"I'm glad they're open again," I said. "A few months ago, the drought was so bad they closed the whole area. There was that yellow **DON'T CROSS** tape over all the entrances."

"We've gotten some rain since then."

"And some storms, too – here, I mean, in the campground. There's a big pine at the top of the road over there," I said, gesturing to my left, north of where The Castle was parked. "Lightning hit it, and brought down the top. Fortunately, no one was camped in that space at the time. The people in the next space over were shaken for a couple of days.

"But they got it cleaned up pretty quickly," I added. "They're good about that here."

"Quick clean up *and* bacon," he said, remembering what I'd told him about the Kamp Kitchen. "Just this side of paradise, then. Do you believe in a paradise?" It wasn't a forced segue, just his natural curiosity.

"Not the way you do," I said, "but we have a sort of equivalent. We call it the Summerland, and it's based on the Celtic model." For the next few minutes, we talked about Wiccan thealogy. He had the general idea, but I clarified a few points for him, just as he clarified a few points about Catholicism for me.

"Did you two decide ... set an appointment for her confession?" I finally asked. I didn't think that question was out of bounds. After all, either I'd have to take Lady Cecelya's ring down to his church, or he'd have to come get it from me.

"In about a week," he said. "She's nervous, but I think I reassured her."

"Facing death is hard enough when you're alive," I said, nodding. "It must be even harder when you've already died once."

"What does Wicca teach about that?"

"Well, the thealogy is that spirits return to the Great Mother, to her unconditional love, and at the same time, we are restored to our prime in the Summerland."

"Two experiences at the same time?"

"The same way you can have two experiences at the same time in a dream, or see things from more than one perspective at a time. Or even," I went on, floundering a little, "like a walking meditation, when you're aware of your surroundings, birds, trees, traffic ... but your mind's on something else."

I got back to my point. "The idea is that we recognize our mistakes, and learn from them, and once we have a good handle on that, we're ready to come back for another round."

"Reincarnation, then."

"Yes, but not necessarily the way Eastern religions understand it. Everyone in their own time, sometimes with vague memories, and sometimes just with ... a sense of calling," I said. "Nature shows us different ways to do the same thing – feed, reproduce, manifest in life – and my Tradition, anyway, teaches that reincarnation happens in various ways, too."

He considered that. "It makes sense," he said. "If it happens to everyone, regardless of belief, I think it will be quite some time before Lady Cecelya's ready to come back."

I nodded my agreement, and then the conversation moved on to other things, mainly beer and cheese.

EIGHTEEN

"Bless me, Father, for I have sinned. It's been over six hundred years since my last confession."

It wasn't hard to imagine how Lady Cecelya would begin her confession. Of course I wasn't hearing it myself, and Father Michael wasn't going to share anything with me, even though I already knew what her sins were.

I knew she'd be going on to say something like, "Before my last confession, I committed mortal sins that I did not confess. I have had an abortion, and I have denied the church and practiced witchcraft ... and I took communion without confessing these sins.

"I'm sure I have committed venial sins as well, but honestly, Father, I don't remember them. Yet for these and all the sins I have committed during my life, I am deeply sorry."

I imagined her saying all these things, but I'd never know for sure unless *she* told me.

That's how confessions go. The sins are different in every case – well, maybe not all that different – but the way they're confessed has been standardized. I thought Lady Cecelya would have to make some modifications to the usual speech, but I was sure she'd manage.

I knew that she'd struggled with contrition. For confession to work, for sins to be forgiven, the penitent has to be truly repentant, and willing to change her life. So Lady Cecelya had two problems: she had to be honest about whether she was really sorry for what she'd done, and she had to cope with not having a life to change.

Was she really sorry for her sins? She did, she said, accept that what she'd done was sinful, in the context of her Catholic beliefs. What she had done wasn't sinful in terms of the witchcraft she'd turned to later in her life, but she seemed to be sorry for turning to it. I understood that: it was for the wrong reason.

I've seen it myself. People come to Wicca because they're mad at their Christian parents, and think the shock of having a witchy child will serve them right. They're much more interested in dramatic ritual and spells than they are in the religion itself.

I think of people like that as occultists, and witches, but not Wiccans – because for them, it's not a religion. They're rebelling against, not coming to. I'm not alone in that assessment, but it's not universal, either.

No one knows exactly what "witchcraft" was like back in Lady Cecelya's day. The Church could only understand Nature worship as Satanic, because they couldn't see any legitimate option to belief in God.

There were, of course, people who could read natural signs – in seasons and weather patterns, in plants, and in animals, wild and domestic, and who had a holistic view of human behavior. They may have practiced Catholicism, but they saw it as a construct, and didn't let it get in the way of what they knew about Nature.

That made them dangerous, because they didn't really recognize the Church's authority. They relied on the knowledge they had from their elders and from their experience, and paid only lip service, not heart service, to the Church.

Heretics, the Church called them, and apostate. Through series of inquisitions, they went after the organized groups first, the Cathars and the Waldensians, but ordinary people were vulnerable, too. At first, penances were light, but the unrepentant were turned over to secular authorities, and that's where burning at the stake came in.

The wise women and cunning men, the people villagers consulted when they, or their livestock, or their crops were sick, they were in mortal peril. If the authorities found out about their potions, and even if their spells included phrases like "by the grace of God," they were accused and tried, tortured and executed.

If their neighbors were unhappy with the results of consultation or conduct, they could complain to the authorities. If neighbors accused neighbors, fingers would be pointed at the old women and old men who lived in the woods and kept to themselves.

These were the witches, we think now. Their rites, as far as we can tell, were nothing like modern Wicca's - but their craft acknowledged the power and spiritual authority of Nature, not the God of golden temples and finely dressed priests. And it was with them, to learn their skills and understandings, that Lady Cecelya consorted.

Did she really take that for a mortal sin? I think she wanted to defy the Church in that respect: some people were praised and rewarded for the same knowledge, cooks and doctors being among them. What was so wrong with knowing the uses of herbs, and what was spiced wine but a potion?

But she'd been taught about the first sin, Adam and Eve's defiance of God in partaking of the knowledge of good and evil. That was Eve's sin, a woman's sin, and here was Lady Cecelya, committing the very same sin, although apples had little to do with it.

But was she sorry for the right reasons? Was she sorry for disappointing God, or sorry because of the potential consequences? If, without worrying about going to Hell, she was sorry for offending her deity, then her contrition was real. If she was only sorry because now she was in trouble, well, that wasn't supposed to count.

Sometimes – and this is true for some of my Wiccan friends, too – I think it would be nice to be Catholic. I didn't grow up in that church, so I have no bad experiences with it. I like the ritual, the grandeur, the incense, the foreign (or at least fancy) language, and the comfort of being told what's right.

As a Wiccan, I am responsible for my behavior, and there's no one to take the consequences for me. Nobody else can take responsibility for any wrong I do; I must make up for my mistakes as best I can, and learn from them, and then move on in better understanding of life, the universe, and everything.

The way my Tradition understands it, the Gods are personifications of life's forces and qualities, and in a way, other-dimensional aspects of myself, because the microcosm is the macrocosm.

There's no one to intercede for me, and no separate-from-everything creator. As they said in the 'sixties, when even the Church was getting a clue, "everything is everything." That's why most Wiccans don't really pray, but do magic: we don't ask some outside entity for help because there is no outside entity. What we do is draw the energy of the universe through ourselves to meet our needs.

Not that we don't have rules or moral guidelines. We follow what we call the Rede: *an ye harm none, do as ye will*, but will doesn't mean want to, it means your deepest calling. "Follow your bliss," Joseph Campbell used to say, bliss being your soul's deepest desire.

And we have the Three-fold Law, which tells us that what we put into the world comes back to us, three-fold. To understand that, you have to know that "three" isn't a literal number, it's a magical number. We interpret it to mean that what we do on one plane, this physical plane where we live, comes back to us from this plane and from all the others as well, in every dimension and in all times.

It's a lot more complicated than our pithy aphorisms make it look – as are the basics of any religion. So Lady Cecelya had a lot of self-examination to tackle before she went to Father Michael and said, "Bless me, Father, for I have sinned."

NINETEEN

I didn't know how much Lady Cecelya would tell me about what Father Michael had said to her.

I had mixed feelings about how much I wanted her to tell me. I did my homework, so I knew most of what she'd said to him. I trusted that she had found contrition in her heart. If she hadn't, she couldn't have finished the rite.

In the world of the living, penances range from the recitation of a Hail Mary through a decade of Rosaries to certain good acts. Sometimes it's a matter of apologizing to someone you've wronged and asking their forgiveness.

Part of her confession was to apologize to God, declaring herself heartily sorry for having offended him. But she couldn't apologize to those she'd wronged in her life – could she?

That gave me something to think about. Could a ghost's penance for an abortion involve finding the soul of the aborted child and asking its forgiveness? Was such a thing even possible? Sometime, maybe, much later, I'd ask Father Michael – hypothetically, of course - about that.

Could she find the souls of her daughter Margaret, the one she thought had suspected her of witchcraft and not confessed what she thought her mother might be up to? Would she have to look in Hell for Margaret, or would that daughter be in Purgatory?

I was pretty sure Lady Cecelya'd stay in Purgatory – assuming that's what her ghostly state was – or go to Hell sooner than she'd apologize to the bishop who directed her husband to kill her, although in theory, she had offended that representative of God by rejecting the Church.

But, I wondered, if the bishop was God's representative, wouldn't an apology to God cover the bishop as well? That question had never come up among my ex-Catholic friends. I trust that was because none of them had gotten to know any bishops well enough to offend them.

The first thing Lacy Cecelya told me was that she would need some help with her penance. She was to say sixty decades – one for each hundred years of her death – of the Rosary. That wasn't as bad as it sounded: the Rosary itself is five decades.

Not surprisingly, though, she no longer remembered all Bible verses. She needed my help to look them up and re-read them. This was a new experience for me. I've read bits of the Bible, of course, but the verses that pertain to the Mysteries represented on the Rosary were not familiar to me. Heck, all I knew about the Rosary before I met Lady Cecelya was that they're called rosaries because originally, the beads were made out of molded rose petals.

Fortunately, the one Father Michael provided for Lady Cecelya was made of turquoise and cedar wood – because I am very allergic to roses. As she became privy to my thoughts about that, she and I realized that I would have to physically count the beads for her, too.

The three of us agreed that she could "say" the rosary in my head; I didn't have to say it out loud for her. But she needed my hands to count the beads.

I knew that Father Michael was kidding when he said helping Lady Cecelya with her penance – part of it, anyway – was my penance for being Pagan.

"Ha," I said. "Never was Christian, much less Catholic."

"I can't absolve you for that," he said, "because it's obvious you're not sorry. But since Vatican Two, I don't have to. Wicca's recognized as a real religion now, and the Church's post-V-Two stand is cooperation with other religions."

"I like your new Pope," I said, and meant it. Francis said you don't have to believe in his god to be a good person, and I appreciate that. I am fortunate to know several other Christians, Catholic and not, who understand that, too.

"So do I," Father Michael said.

We didn't have the conversation about Wicca's conception of deity being quite different than the Abrahamic one. He was wise enough not to trot out the "all religions believe the same thing in different words" cliché, so I didn't have to find a nice way to disagree.

The older I get, the more courage – if that's the right word – I have to let people know that no, Wicca's Mother Goddess is not just Yahweh in drag. Luckily, the older I get, the more nice ways I can find to say so. But it was nice not to need to say so to Father Michael. With him, there were other priorities, and unlike Lady Cecelya, I didn't have six hundred years to address them.

●

It was good, I thought, that Lady Cecelya remembered as much as she did about praying the Rosary. I had to make the sign of the cross for her, but I did so while holding her ring, so that both of us felt it was she doing it, not me.

She remembered the *Apostles' Creed* on her own, and the *Our Father*, and the *Hail Mary*. The *Glory Be* wasn't hard for her either. I suspected – and she later confirmed – that Father Michael had reminded her of these prayers. That was kind of him, for her sake and for mine.

It was the Mysteries she needed help with. There used to be three: the Joyful Mysteries to remember Christ's birth, the Sorrowful Mysteries to remember his passion and death, and the Glorious Mysteries, focusing on Jesus' resurrection. There are Bible verses to recite for each of them.

Father Michael told Lady Cecelya about the Mysteries of Light, about which she knew nothing. Pope John Paul the Second added them centuries after Lady Cecelya's death – but she did remember which Bible verses Father Michael had told her went with those, so we had no trouble looking them up.

I had a copy of the New Testament from a friend of mine who's a Presbyterian minister, and thanks to the Internet, I knew before Lady Cecelya did which verses she'd need to see through my eyes. I marked them all with sticky flags from the local office supply, so it was just a matter of turning to the right pages.

Usually, nothing is recited on the center medallion. On the Rosary from Father Michael, that was a heart-shaped turquoise bead, to match the large beads that began each decade. But Lady Cecelya chose to recite the Beatitudes over the heart.

Lady Cecelya thought – as many modern Catholics do – that it would be a good idea to add the *Fatima Prayer*, too. "O, my Jesus, forgive us our sins, save us from the fires of Hell, and lead all souls to Heaven, especially those in most need of Thy mercy. Amen." Thealogical differences aside, I couldn't disagree with her.

When we were still writing things down – we didn't much, anymore – she'd questioned me once about spelling thealogy with an **a** when I was talking about my religion, and with an **o** when we were discussing hers.

I think she thought it was unnecessary, but she accepted my explanation that our primary deity is female, and in Greek, the origin of the word, that would be *thea*, not *theo*. She was from another era, after all, and still felt that "man" and "men" could mean women too, though she admitted that in practice, it didn't always.

She had a good memory. I looked once at most of the verses she needed to read, and she remembered them after that. The *Hail, Holy Queen* we had to look at twice. I was impressed. It took me weeks, making up tunes and singing them in the shower, to memorize my Trad's liturgies.

TWENTY

I couldn't think of anything else while Lady Cecelya was saying her Rosary.

So I thought about the prayers too. I didn't want to distract Lady Cecelya from her penance, but I couldn't help translating for myself.

Lady Cecelya would tell me, I thought, if my meditations disturbed her prayers. By this time, all she needed was to borrow my vision. She and I had learned to keep our thoughts separate when we wanted to. In prayer on her Rosary, she was very tightly concentrated, and I let her move my fingers along the beads, so I was free to follow my own thoughts.

I believe that the Universe is our Mother, and that I am both her child and her self. I could have gone on about the Horned God, who is the Celtic stag of seven tines, the salmon of knowledge, who is both hunter and prey.

But as it often does, acknowledging the Goddess as all that is eternal and generative led me to recall stunning images of nebulas, and the feelings I get when people's hearts and minds are united in beautiful music, and when I learn of people doing wonderful, gentle things for each other and the rest of life.

You, who are the beauty of the green Earth and the white Moon among the stars, and the mystery of the waters ... the soul of the universe who gives life ... I answer your call. From you all things proceed, and unto you all things return. You have been with me from the beginning ....

Following the form of the *Our Father* Lady Cecelya was chanting, that was my paraphrase of the *Charge of the Goddess*, Wicca's most belovéd liturgical piece.

I found myself hailing the Great Mother, affirming that the God – my god, the Horned God, all that dies and is reborn – was with her, and she with him. We are all the fruit of her womb, and all of us blessed with the wonders of mortality and the power of reincarnation. We are not sinners, but yes, we have her love – the Gods' love – now and at the hour of our death.

Dream-like, the rhythm of Lady Cecelya's praying the Rosary took me between the worlds, as I suspect it is meant to do. Catholics no doubt understand it differently - they certainly don't talk about being between the worlds - but all prayer and meditation brings us to an interface with our deities.

Penance, I realized, isn't punishment, not really. It's reaffirmation, reconnection. And that can be hard work, just like any homeward journey can be arduous. I guess that's what makes it seem like punishment.

From my Wiccan perspective, though, it's not punishment, it's authenticity. This kind of contemplation connects with our own true self, and thus with the truth of our gods. I don't know that that's how Lady Cecelya, or Father Michael, or his bishop, see it, but that's how it works for me.

It can be frightening to get in touch with our authentic selves. It requires a great and very personal effort to touch our own souls. Oddly, it can be harder to accept what is good about ourselves than to acknowledge our flaws. But when we do, we can make the wonderful discovery that our gods do love us, *and* that we are worthy of their love.

That's not vanity. That's respect for the part of us that is divine ... and that's what I mean by translation.

My thealogy and cosmology are different than Lady Cecelya's and Father Michael's, but the peace and freedom I feel when I am touching that part of my soul that is the Goddess, I believe that's what we all feel when we let ourselves feel our deity's embrace.

It was dark when Lady Cecelya finished her decades. We were both exhausted, in a good way. I could tell that she felt better, and I felt fulfilled as well. Lady Cecelya, I guessed, would want some down time, so I put her ring back in the box. Me, I needed to ground, so I put some bacon-wrapped scallops in the microwave and opened a beer.

●

I wasn't surprised when Lady Cecelya confided that saying the Rosary wasn't her only penance.

"I need to keep someone else from making my mistakes," she said.

"Okay. How are you going to do that?"

"Father Michael said it wouldn't help to turn you away from your faith, even though some people call it witchcraft," she said.

"Just as well," I told her.

"Father Michael said you wouldn't be persuaded from your faith. My witchcraft wasn't faith," she added.

"Ahh," I said, and tried to keep my thoughts away from the fact that I'd already known that.

"So I need to keep someone else from aborting a child."

I'd have seen that coming if I'd thought about it hard enough. I'm solid with "my body, my choice," and while I hope anyone thinking about abortion will consider all the options, I wouldn't dream of telling someone else what to do in that regard.

I've escorted women into abortion clinics, shielding them from the so-called pro-life protestors. I know it's never an easy decision. I know it's scary, and something a woman never forgets. Have I ever had an abortion? None of your business.

The idea of helping Lady Cecelya persuade someone to do her faith's duty wasn't my idea of right ... but neither was refusing to help her do what she felt she must. My dilemma was that in our faith, it's not okay to impose our will on other people, so denying someone a lawful choice because it's not the choice we'd make, that's a bad thing.

I considered that to show someone that there are alternatives to abortion – assuming no medical need to have one – isn't a bad thing. Showing people all their choices and helping them make the best one work, that's a good thing, as long as we let them decide what the best choice for them is.

And: my religious duty is to do what I will – pursue my soul's calling – as long as I harm none. Knowing that Lady Cecelya couldn't accomplish her task without my help made my refusal harmful.

Or did it? Couldn't Father Michael help her? I could bring him Lady Cecelya's ring, and he could take it, and her with it, to .... Planned Parenthood? A shelter? Where would Lady Cecelya find someone to talk out of having an abortion?

Maybe a school. Father Michael could get Lady Cecelya's ring into a Catholic school, certainly, but if he did that with a mind to letting her talk someone into keeping the baby, he'd be admitting that there were Catholic girls considering abortion. He wasn't parochial, though, so maybe he knew that could be true.

If I were taking her, I'd still have to answer the same question: where would we go? What could Father Michael or I say to anyone? "Hello, I've brought a ghost who needs to talk one of your young women out of having an abortion" didn't seem like the kind of thing that would get either of us through any doors.

Maybe the Youth Center ... but again, how? It seemed to me that Father Michael might have better luck visiting than I would. I had no professional or clerical status – and no degree in counseling. Even being an ordained priestess wouldn't help me wander in unannounced.

I supposed I'd have to come up with a program, maybe a two- or three-part program, to present. Something about Wicca's inclusiveness, to offer another religious option for people. That would take time to prepare, and time to pitch – and there was no guarantee my proposal would be accepted.

"We could just go downtown," Lady Cecelya suggested. "Walk around. You're pretty good at reading people. Maybe we'd just ... find someone who needed to talk about an unexpected, unwanted pregnancy."

"We can try that," I said.

A few weeks earlier, I would have been unwilling to take Lady Cecelya out into the world. She'd felt unstable to me then, and angry, and she was capable of lashing out destructively. But since she'd found out there was a chance for redemption, she'd been calmer.

I liked to think my not just jamming her back in the box and burning it or something had helped heal her. But Father Michael's counsel, whatever it had been, had been even more restorative.

"I don't mind if it takes a while," Lady Cecelya said.

"Okay."

I was wanting to move on, too, albeit heading to New Mexico instead of Heaven, but that plan had already been delayed by a couple of weeks, so what was a few more days? I glanced at the calendar hanging by the door. The Moon was almost full, and that gave me an idea.

Lady Cecelya had sworn off witchcraft, so I doubted that she'd be comfortable with magic, but I thought it might help. My gods don't mind working with other gods, and the Second Vatican Council had come out in favor of Catholics working with followers of other faiths, so maybe it would be alright.

"You want to do magic?"

"I do," I answered. "You don't have to be involved."

"But if you're doing it for me," Lady Cecelya said, proving she'd been paying attention to my thoughts and the things I said out loud, "don't you need my permission?"

"If it's on your behalf, yes. If it's for me, no."

"How would it be for you?"

"I want to go to New Mexico; I want circumstances to be right for that to happen. If I do magic to that end, it's about me, not you."

"Except that mine is the main circumstance that's keeping you here," she countered ... and she was right. My plan was definitely putting me in a grey area.

"Maybe not the only circumstance, but yes, the main one. I want to help you, my lady, but I want to live my life, too."

"I understand," she said. "I was angry about my choices being taken away. Now that I have a chance for my life to end well, I don't want to spoil yours."

"It's not so much that you're spoiling my life," I said, realizing I'd probably sounded like that's what I meant. "It's that I can't take responsibility for yours. I know you have certain limitations – and they they're not the result of your own choices. And in my religion," I said, "when we have problems that we can't solve by mundane means, we work magic to – "

"Make happen what you want to have happen," she finished.

"Ultimately. But the mechanism of magic is to ...." I've explained this many times, in many ways, but I was always looking for a new way to put it. "The two of us can think of a few ways for you to accomplish your task," I started again. "I can take you out somewhere, somewhere specific or just ... onto the sidewalk, where you might meet someone who could benefit from your counsel. Or Father Michael could take you. But those are the only ways *we* can think of to do this."

"Yes," Lady Cecelya said.

"Magic will ... maybe create, or maybe just let us be aware of more ways for it to happen. Something we haven't thought of, or something we can't do on our own, will happen, and you'll be able to perform your penance, and I'll be able to go to New Mexico."

"I think I understand," Lady Cecelya said. "Father Michael said your religion is accepted now, so if you can't object to prayer, maybe I shouldn't object to the magic you do. Your witchcraft feels very different from mine."

"I don't even call mine witchcraft," I reminded her. "The magic I do is in the context of a religion. It's bound by rules. It challenges me to be more creative, and it requires me to be sure that what I do honors what is sacred."

"You do not hide it from the authorities."

"No, I don't. I like privacy when I work, just as you like privacy when you pray, but no, I don't hide my faith."

"Father Michael knows you are ... Wiccan," she said. I think she started to say "a witch," but she wanted to make the distinction.

"Yes, he does."

"Do you think he knows that you do magic?"

"I think he probably does, yes."

"If he didn't want you to help me, or not help me with the magic he knows you do, he would have made that clear when he gave me my penance," she mused. I didn't think she was asking my opinion about that, so I didn't say anything. She needed to find her own comfort level here.

"I said in my confession that I was sorry for offending God with my witchcraft," she said. "And I am. But what you do – what is in your mind about what you do – is not like the witchcraft I was taught.

"Casting spells is forbidden in the Old Testament," she went on; it just happened that I could hear her talking to herself. I probably should have put her ring down and not eavesdropped, but I kept my fingers on it. "But Jesus made a new covenant ...."

"Lady Cecelya," I interrupted when I could hear her distress mounting, "if it's any help to you, when I work magic, what I am doing – what I see myself doing – is working with the energy of life. I'm not depriving anyone else, and when I have what I need, I replace that energy in other ways.

"In some ways, it is no different from taking my portion of the meal from the dish in the center of the table. There's still plenty left for everyone else, and I have no intention of depriving anyone. But unless I take some from the bowl, my plate will be empty and I will go hungry."

"Then the question I have to answer," Lady Cecelya said, "is whether I should eat from your plate. And for that answer, I will need to pray."

TWENTY-ONE

Sometime during the night, one of those times when I was almost sleeping, it occurred to me.

Respecting Lady Cecelya's religion, and acknowledging her obligations to it, didn't mean I had to repress mine. I got over the resentment pretty quickly: it wasn't her fault I'd been holding back on her account.

In the morning, it was warm enough that I could sit outside, and cool enough that I could take a cup of tea with me. And my Tarot deck.

I'm not a professional reader, and not even a regular reader of the cards. But now and then, I do find a three-card draw useful. It's not that the cards tell me what to do, it's that they show me a new perspective to take on whatever I'm considering. And I definitely needed a new perspective.

Lady Cecelya wasn't involved in this. I was well aware that this was, in the biblical sense, divination, and expressly forbidden, at least in the Old Testament. Then again, I wasn't trying to divine the future, because that's not what the cards do. They only suggest what to expect if things keep going the way they're headed. But as far as Lady Cecelya was concerned – and it was probably true for Father Michael, too – reading my cards was a big no-no.

The thing is, none of us are obligated to follow other people's religions. That's what the First Amendment of our Constitution is about: *Congress shall make no law respecting an establishment of religion, or prohibiting the free exercise thereof* .... Reading Tarot cards isn't part of every Wiccan's practice, but it's part of mine.

A three-card draw is generally a horizontal line of three cards, laid out from left to right. The one on the left represents the past, the one in the middle is the present, and the one on the right is about the future. Not the immutable future, but what's likely to happen if something in the present doesn't change.

The cards I drew – after a good shuffle, of course – were the four of Wands, the Ace of Pentacles, and the five of Swords.

I read the four of Wands as, more or less, mental stability. And yes, that was a fair call on my life BLC – before Lady Cecelya. The Ace of Pentacles refers to survival and first causes, which also seemed appropriate.

The last card, the "future" card, was the five of Swords. Swords stand for action, to over-simplify. Power, authority, urgency. Fives are about struggle and separation. What this told me was that we were on the right track. Struggle seemed inevitable, and separation – at least of Lady Cecelya from this plane, and me from Arizona – was the goal.

I decided to draw two more cards, laying them above and below the five of Swords. Maybe that would give me some ideas about how to proceed. The bottom card should reveal, or at least confirm, something about the foundation of the situation, and the top one might suggest a way forward.

The bottom card was the two of Wands. Concepts, processes ... balance and polarity. Well, Lady Cecelya had certainly been dealing with all of that, and for a lot longer than I'd known her.

The top card was the Queen of Cups – reversed. Cups are mysteries and emotions (among other things). Queens are representative of good women, honest and devoted women. Traditionally, a Queen reversed is someone duplicitous, but in this case, my intuition was that the reversal showed Lady Cecelya's confusion.

I drew two more cards and laid them on either side of the upside-down Queen. Behind all the confusion was transformation; ahead was disgrace and disquiet. This was not only discomfiting, it was unhelpful.

Maybe I hadn't been focused enough when I shuffled the cards. I got myself started on a little mantra, to some tune I no longer remember: How shall I go forward? How shall we proceed? and then I shuffled again.

The first card of the next three-card draw was the seven of Pentacles, reversed. People disagree about this card's meaning; I took it, in this case, as my contentment with my life – and as Lady Cecelya's life turned upside down.

The center card, representing the here-and-now, was the nine of Swords. It's kind of a scary card to see – someone waking from a bad dream, or maybe too sad to sleep, with a screen of swords behind them. But nines are completion. Fair enough: completing what was going on now did involve some fear and sorrow. It didn't mean things wouldn't be alright in the end.

The third card was the three of Swords, reversed. It meant alienation, error, and confusion. Oh, dear.

But that would be the outcome only if something didn't change right now. I laid one more card over the center, hoping it would suggest what change I could make. I got the eight of Cups. Great: experience and inspiration. Yes, cards, thank you. That's what I'm asking for.

Once more into the deck, and the next card up was the three of Wands. The best I could make of that was that I should maybe involve Father Michael. Threes are about synthesis and groups, and we were already a sort of group of three.

Then I thought that Father Michael was already involved. He'd given Lady Cecelya a penance, and she still needed to get into somebody else's head and heart. As I was the one helping Lady Cecelya accomplish her penance, maybe she and I and the woman we had yet to meet were the group of three the card might be referencing.

I had another idea then, and reshuffled the deck to see if the cards – really my own subconscious – had anything encouraging to say about that.

That's the thing about cards. If I'm confused when I read for myself, the cards won't do much but reflect my confusion. But in drawing cards to my budding idea, I was really just thinking aloud, if you call the soft slap of cards on a table "aloud."

The first card this time was the six of Swords, reversed. For the first time in ages, I consulted the little book that comes with every Tarot deck. Declaration and confession. That was a reasonable card to have in the "past" position.

The second was the four of Wands again, but this time reversed. Prosperity! Things might be looking up in this reading. Maybe my idea was a good one.

The third card was the two of Pentacles, and *not* reversed. Obstacles again. I studied the card more closely. The traditional interpretations come from a different time, and people's underlying assumptions about the world have changed since this deck was created in 1910.

The card is a young man – quite a jolly one, dressed in reds and oranges – very focused on juggling two pentacles connected in a lemniscate, the infinity symbol. The young man has one foot off the ground, which suggests to me that he's dancing, likely in rhythm with his juggling.

Behind him is a flat horizon, and over the horizon – maybe a beach - are sea-swells, with one ship riding a crest and another visible at the side of a trough. As I see it, those are more references to rhythm and balance.

Looking at the card that time, it seemed significant to me that the ship that was higher in the background was behind the lower pentagram, and the lower ship was behind the higher pentagram. The edge of the sea was straight, and that straight was the sum of the two moving elements in the card.

I thought about this and what it might mean in our situation. I drew one more card. It was the Wheel of Fortune, reversed. I made a little victory noise then, because that stood for increase and abundance. That encouraged me to think that my idea would work.

It would also mean bidding Lady Cecelya adieu sooner rather than later.

TWENTY-TWO

I came back in and puttered around for a while.

There are still household chores to do, even if the household is small, and while I was doing mine, I considered how to share my idea with Lady Cecelya. I didn't think she'd like it, and I didn't think she'd care for the way I came up with it, either.

The idea didn't come directly from the cards, of course. There are no cards that say "do this" or "go there." The cards suggest relationships between the person consulting them and the rest of the world, whether that's the mundane world or the spiritual one, or both. New perspectives, or reminders of old ones, is what the cards present.

My readings only took me out of my frustration long enough to let another idea, one of my own, get its foot in my mind's door. Studying each card often does that for me, whether or not I'm seeing the same things in the card that the artist did, or that other readers do, for that matter.

The problem we were trying to solve was how to put Lady Cecelya in touch with someone who needed her advice about an unwanted pregnancy. It wasn't practical to take her - take her ring - to places where we might find unhappily pregnant young women. Wandering around downtown Flag until we happened to bump into someone who wanted to blurt something like that out to a total stranger didn't seem all that practical either.

How else could we get Lady Cecelya near enough to someone who needed her voice in their head? How could we get her ring into the hands of someone she could counsel?

The idea I had was to take Lady Cecelya's ring – just the ring, not the box or the lock of her hair – to a thrift shop. Donate it. Let the right person be drawn to it.

Lord knows – yes, sometimes we call our god "Lord" – that's happened to me often enough. I've found some amazing things at thrift shops, some amazing Pagan things. They seem to call me, though not the same way Lady Cecelya talks in my head. It seemed likely to me that this method, which didn't involve any magic except whatever blessings Lady Cecelya had accrued for herself, could work.

"I do not understand what a thrift shop is."

"It's a place where well-off people bring things they aren't using any more, so that poorer people can buy them and use them."

"Is it … charity?"

"Not exactly," I tried to explain. "It looks like a regular shop, but prices are less. People still pay for what they want."

"A market, but with things other than food."

"Yes."

"For poor people."

"Or thrifty people, like me."

"You want to take me – take the ring – to one of these, and hope someone planning an abortion buys it so I can talk to her."

"Yes." I thought it was a good sign that it still sounded like a workable idea when I talked about it out loud.

"I'm not sure," she said.

"Understandable. Why don't we go to the thrift shop I have in mind, and just look around a little, so you can see the place first. Then we can talk about it again."

"You won't leave the ring there?"

"Not this time, no. Not unless we decide together."

After a pause, she said "Thank you. I do want to complete my penance, with hope of getting to Heaven," she said. "But leaving here, leaving you and Father Michael, that will be like dying again."

"Only this time you won't have to be afraid," I said.

"No," she said. "I'm not afraid. But I'm having a good time. Is it a sin to want to stay here a little longer?"

"Not as far as I'm concerned," I said. New Mexico could wait. The brew pub I liked in Las Cruces wasn't going anywhere. In fact, High Desert Brewing would be a great place to raise a glass to Lady Cecelya's success, assuming she agreed to try this plan and it worked.

We went down to Savers that afternoon. I hadn't worn her ring in quite some time, but carrying it around the thrift store would have looked funny at best and suspicious at worst. I'd tried wearing it as a pendant, but that didn't work as well as putting it on my finger.

I crossed the parking lot fairly quickly. Lady Cecelya seemed to take modern traffic in stride, and she did think it was nice that there was no horse poop on the ground here. But it was the shop itself she wanted to see.

The Savers in Flagstaff is on Highway 89, in the Safeway complex. I've always liked it. It's big, and they have a wide variety of items to choose from. It's not like a regular store, of course: you can't find the same dress or pants in various sizes. I think of it as everything being one-of-a-kind, unless someone's gotten rid of a set of bridesmaid's dresses or something.

It's true of most thrift shops that the aisles could be a little wider, but the inconvenience of getting past another shopper with your cart is well-balanced, I think, by the more clothes the narrower aisle make room for. Lady Cecelya was suitably impressed.

"I am going to do a little shopping while we're here," I told her. "But let's go look at the jewelry counter first. That's where your ring would go."

It was good luck, I thought, that there were a couple of women looking at the necklaces and earrings under the glass. There's a lot of jewelry out where people can pick it up and put it in their carts without a clerk's help, but the very nicest pieces are in display cabinets so that no one can make off with them.

"Are those real pearls?" She sounded astonished. We were looking at a particularly nice two-stranded necklace of white and black pearls.

"Cultured," I said. The black ones were slightly irregular, with three white ones between them.

"Very," she said, in an accent I could recognize as posh. It made me chuckle, and it pleased me that she could make fun of her own social status like that.

"A cultured pearl is one that people have helped the oyster make," I said. "It's real, but it's not left to chance."

"Ahh," she said. "And are those cultured diamonds and rubies?" My finger twitched as if to point at some earrings in the case.

"Glass," I said. "But they're beautiful pieces, aren't they?"

We were alone at the jewelry counter by this time, so before a clerk came over to ask if there was anything we wanted to look at more closely, I turned away toward the aisles of blouses and tank tops.

It had taken Lady Cecelya some time to get used to modern clothing styles. Jeans and tee-shirts shocked her at first, but shorts were what really rattled her, even more than women in sleeveless tops. She didn't believe me the first time I told her that no, nobody was out in their underwear.

She was also surprised to see people of color. The darkest-skinned people she'd ever seen before were heavily-tanned field-hands. I was glad that I could explain the wide range of skin colors in a way that didn't make racism another sin for her confess.

I make my thrift-shop rounds slowly, and if I see a worker adding items to a rack, I go back and check those, too. I don't go very often, so when I do, I want to be sure not to miss anything. There are so many things crowded together that it pays to run my hand along the line of hangers to free up anything that's gotten tucked behind.

Lady Cecelya was, fortunately, confined to her ring. If she'd been independent, she'd have been like a small child, into everything, touching, running, and playing in the hems of garments. As it was, she couldn't stop talking about all the colors and patterns she saw on the shirts and skirts I looked at.

It took a little longer than half an hour for me to check everything that interested me. I didn't bother with the books, for instance, because I have no bookshelves. The few books I have are stored in baskets in doored compartments, and for everything else, I have an e-reader. We didn't look at men's clothes, either. The only register open when I was ready to pay for my finds was the one closest to the jewelry counter, and the line was long enough that we could take one last look while we waited.

TWENTY-THREE

I kept my eyes on the counter, so Lady Cecelya could gawk to her heart's content.

But as the check-out line moved and I took another step toward the cashier, we gasped at the same time. If we could have, we'd have exchanged an O.M.G. look.

Leaning over the jewelry case was a young woman, maybe fifteen or sixteen. She had one hand over her abdomen, and with the other kept brushing her bangs out of her face.

Would I have reacted the same way if I hadn't been involved with Lady Cecelya? I hope so, but if I'm honest, probably not. I probably will the next time, though.

Still hearing Lady Cecelya sort of gasping with excitement in my mind, I stepped out of line and went to stand beside the girl at the jewelry counter.

"Pretty, aren't they?" I said.

"Beautiful."

"I can't afford any of them either," I said.

She smiled slightly. "I'd be happy if I could get a new pair of jeans."

"You know what?" I said. "Let's make that happen." I was talking to Lady Cecelya, too, and I could feel that she knew it.

"What?"

"I have a little extra cash today," I said. "Let's go find you some jeans. And maybe a shirt or two."

She looked me over. I don't look threatening. I'm not very tall, and I'm not flashy. I don't have a sinister smile. My hair is mostly grey now.

"Why? What do I have to do for that?"

"Because people should help each other, and all you have to do is ... sometime help somebody else when you can."

"Really, lady?"

It felt funny when she addressed me that way. My religious title is Lady, but this girl couldn't know that. I knew she meant "ma'am," but it didn't matter much: I feel funny when people call me "ma'am," too. In my head, Lady Cecelya wondered how the girl knew about *her*.

"My name's Seelie," I said. "I live in a trailer a few miles north of here. What's your name?"

"Bonnie," the girl said. "I don't live anywhere at the moment – but that's okay," she added quickly. "It's warm. But when – " She stopped herself.

"When it gets cold again?" It does get cold in Flagstaff. It snows.

"When the baby comes," she whispered.

"I think I know somebody who can help you with all of that," I said, hoping she understood that I wasn't judging her, and hoping I didn't sound gleeful. "And right now, I can help you with some clothes, and maybe a few other things."

"Somebody who can help? Do you mean a clinic? For an abortion? Because that's what I want. I can't take care of a baby."

"Hard decision," I acknowledged. I wanted to let her know there were other options, but I couldn't do Lady Cecelya's job for her. She'd been given this opportunity, and I needed to let her take it. "But no, that's not what I meant."

"Are you ... are you my guardian angel, Seelie?" She looked and sounded like an eight-year-old child just then.

"Maybe so," I said. "Or maybe just a nice lady buyin' you a pair of jeans."

"Maybe so," Lady Cecelya echoed me.

•

Neither Lady Cecelya nor I let ourselves think too much about what meeting Bonnie meant for our future. Bonnie's future was enough to focus on for the moment. We rolled through the thrift shop again, this time with a cart, and we were on a mission.

Bonnie wasn't showing yet, but she probably would be soon. We picked out one pair of regular jeans, and I snuck a couple of maternity pairs in, too. "Could you use another couple of tops?"

"Yes," she said. Her voice was soft. I'm sure she knew that she didn't smell very good. When we were done shopping, I'd take her for something to eat, and then to a shelter. And then I'd call Father Michael.

We headed down the women's tops aisles, and with my encouragement, she picked out two or three. I was pleased to see that a dusky violet seemed to be her favorite color. The ring would look good with those shirts.

That thought jolted Lady Cecelya a little. She was a little dazed again when she realized that I wasn't planning on bringing Bonnie back to The Castle.

While Bonnie was going through the long-sleeved shirts, I silently affirmed to Lady Cecelya that "Yes, our plan has changed. I think you'll be going with Bonnie this afternoon. If she'll accept your ring as a memento of our serendipitous meeting."

"But ...."

"My lady," I said, taking the stern mental tone she'd come to know, "meeting someone like Bonnie was our goal – your goal. With her, you have a chance to complete your penance, and for your absolution to manifest. Meeting Bonnie is a sign that it's time."

"I know. But I'm still afraid."

"I understand. But we've talked about this before. Taking the first step is always hard. But remember the glories of your heaven. Trust Father Michael and trust your god," I said.

"I do," she said. But I could feel her shaking.

Once Bonnie had picked out a few blouses, we went to look at shoes. She found some tennies in her size, but no sandals to replace the falling-apart ones she was wearing. They sell new socks at this Savers, so we got her a couple of pairs of those, too.

"Now," I said, "I know you could make do with carrying these things around in the bag they'll give us at the register, but I want you to have a back pack or something for your stuff."

"I still don't know why you're doing this for me," she said.

"Because somebody was good to me once, long ago, and I'm paying it forward." It was the truth. I've never been in Bonnie's situation, but a lot of people have been very nice – gratuitously nice – to me over the years, and I think we do need to pay such kindness forward.

"My dad's new wife doesn't like me, and she'd be really upset if she knew I was pregnant. My mom already kicked me out, so ... so I really appreciate this," she said.

I wanted to hug her, but that seemed like going too far, at least in public, so I didn't. Instead, I led her to the area of the shop where the ladies purses mingle with waist packs, tote bags, back packs, and a few rolling carry-on bags.

She giggled at a couple of packs with cartoon characters on them, and although I didn't say anything, I was glad she didn't choose one of those. I wanted her to move toward grown-up dignity, not back toward the childhood she could never reclaim. That was none of my business, though, and if she'd wanted the, what, Hello Spongebob? one, I'd have gotten if for her.

She ended up with a medium-sized maroon piece of luggage, the kind with an extending handle and wheels that will turn in any direction. It looked almost new, and correspondingly pricey, but it was worth it. It would hold everything we'd gotten today, and more.

There was room for a blanket, and I thought she should have one. As we made our way back across the shop, I saw one or two other things I thought she could use – including a wide-brimmed hat - and put those in the cart too.

The cashier was happy to put one bunch of stuff in the rolling case, and my stuff in one of the non-woven, not-plastic bags most thrift shops use now. Bonnie was surprised again when I told her to follow me to the truck.

"You're not going to tell me you don't want lunch," I said.

She took a deep breath, knowing that she should wonder whether I was some innocent-looking pervert, but wanting to trust her feeling that I wasn't. "No," she said. She straightened up a little, and said, "I'm starving."

I could understand how a kid like Bonnie would have trouble trusting her judgement right now. Maybe she'd thought the baby's father loved her. But equally likely, she hadn't known she could, or hadn't been able, to say no. It didn't matter to me. There was no blame in my faith and none in my heart for her.

Lady Cecelya was, of course, sympathetic.

We went to Arby's for lunch even though it's way across town because it's my favorite fast-food place. I'm a sucker for the gyros. Bonnie wanted a bacon cheese-burger, and that's what she got, with plenty of fries and a shake. We ate sitting in the bed of my truck, our legs dangling over the tailgate, under the shade of a tree in the parking lot. Her new hat looked good on her.

"Remember that one tee you got, the long-sleeved one with the V-neck," I said.

"Mmm," she responded. Her mouth was full.

"That's a really pretty color. It looks really nice on you. And – well, I know this sounds silly," I went on, "but I'd like you to have something to remember me by."

She looked up, swallowed her bite, and said, "How can you think I'd ever forget all of this?"

"Oh, I know," I said, "but clothes get old, and you'll replace them, and even the suitcase will wear out one day. Or you'll pass it on to someone else in need. I want you to have something of mine, something you won't ever have to replace, or need to give away."

She took refuge in her burger again. "That does sound kinda goofy," she said before she took another bite.

"Will you humor me?"

"What do you want to give me?"

"This ring," I said. "I know you like pretty jewelry, and now you have at least one shirt that this matches. Can we see if it fits?"

Lady Cecelya was tingling in my brain, not articulating her feelings at all. But it didn't feel like she was trying to stop me.

TWENTY-FOUR

It had to go on Bonnie's index finger, but of course the ring fit her.

The various gods involved in this weren't the kind to bring Bonnie to us and then keep the plan from working. I knew that it might occur to Bonnie to hock the ring for cash, but I didn't think she would. Too trusting? I might be, sometimes, but this time I was sure ... and as it turned out, Bonnie didn't let me down.

After lunch, I took Bonnie to the Family Help Center. I had to call first, because places that take in victims of domestic violence don't put their addresses on the web. We got there in about half an hour, and I got Bonnie checked in with them. She didn't have a phone, but I gave her my number anyway. I left my name and number at the desk, too.

Driving home without the ring, and without Lady Cecelya in my head, was a little disorienting. I still had the maze-box, and the lock of her hair, and I was pretty sure that if she really wanted to, she could find her way back to me.

The only thing that really nagged at me was that I had no way of knowing how all of this would turn out.

When would Lady Cecelya introduce herself to Bonnie, and how? Would she be able to convince Bonnie to keep her baby? Was Bonnie healthy enough to survive a full-term pregnancy and birth? It saddened me that I'd probably never know.

When I got home, I gave myself a few minutes to gaze nostalgically at the maze-box. I touched the lock of Lady Cecelya's hair by way of bidding her farewell, and closed the box. I emptied the rice and put the dish that had held it in the sink.

And then I called Father Michael to let him know how my afternoon – and Lady Cecelya – had gone.

●

I hadn't told Father Michael anything about my plan to donate Lady Cecelya's ring to the thrift shop in hopes of someone who'd listen to her counsel would find it. So I started there.

"How did she feel about that?"

"Muddled," I said, realizing that was exactly the right word. "So we decided to go down to Savers so she could see what the place was like, so it wouldn't be another unknown to her.

"The plan was to come back to The Castle and talk about it some more, so she could have time to think about it. But while we were there, we ran into Bonnie. We both knew the minute we saw her that she was Lady Cecelya's opportunity. A boon."

"So you ...?"

"I struck up a conversation with her, and ended up buying her a few things – she couldn't afford anything at all. I think she came in just for the air conditioning. After that, we had lunch, and I dropped her off at Family Help. That's where Bonnie and Lady Cecelya are now, as far as I know."

"So you gave Bonnie the amethyst ring," Father Michael concluded.

"Yes. I told her I wanted her to have something of mine to remember me by. It wasn't really mine, but Lady Cecelya knew what I was thinking, and she didn't try to stop me."

"But ...?"

I grinned, even though he couldn't see me smile. "But now I'm a little sad that I'll never know how it all turns out. I won't know how Bonnie and Lady Cecelya get along, or whether Cecelya can persuade Bonnie to keep the baby, and whether she'll make it to Heaven.

"I wouldn't even know what that would look like," I said, thinking more about it as I spoke to the priest. "Would there be a ... a glory-ball suddenly rise up to the sky and disappear? Sort of like in the old paintings?"

"Good question," Father Michael said. "I expect that people of different sensitivities to that sort of thing would see it differently – and some not at all." He paused. "An ascension like the Old Masters depicted would be something to see, alright. We can only hope it would be visible to us."

Unhelpfully, I nodded.

"I'll give Family Help a call, and let them know that I'm available if she – or any of their clients – want to talk. I take it she hasn't got anybody else."

"She said she can't stay with either of her parents, so no, she doesn't. Just you and me."

"But how much longer will you be at the KOA?" he asked me. "I thought you wanted to go out to New Mexico. Las Cruces, wasn't it?"

"It was," I said. "It is. But I'll be here a few more days yet. I need to make reservations at the KOA over there."

"All this has left you feeling pretty out of control, eh?"

I laughed with him. "Yes, but I'm inclined to reserve ahead anyway. I've never liked the idea of getting stuck by the side of the road or at a second-rate campground. I like my full hook-ups and pull-through sites. And I like being part of a community of campers with a mix of full-timers and vacationers."

"Fair enough. I thought about a hermitage," he told me, "but that really wasn't my calling. Pastoral work, that's what I like. Even at the gym, I'm always a priest."

I was nodding again, and then remembered I was on the phone and needed to speak. "When I was working full-time, I met people who needed pastoral advice," I said, "and I gave it. I was someone they could vent to, someone who didn't judge, someone who assumed they were worthy when they were feeling bad about themselves."

"Exactly. So now you wish you could know what happens to Lady Cecelya – and to Bonnie."

"I do," I said. "I know I can't, so I'll just have to trust in my gods, as you trust in yours, that everything goes well for them both."

"Are you going to cast any spells to that end?"

"I'd like to, but one of our rules is not to do magic for other people, even magic for their success, without their permission. I didn't talk to Bonnie about it at all, and the little bit Lady Cecelya and I talked about it left me with the impression that she'd rather I didn't."

"I think you're right about Lady Cecelya," he said.

"That's not going to stop me from wishing them both the best of everything, and wishing hard," I said. "You're going to pray for them?"

"I am. I know Lady Cecelya wants me to, and ... my Church doesn't restrict me from praying for anyone."

"Would you pray for me even if I asked you not to?" I had to ask.

There was a long silence. "Are you asking me not to?"

"Are you praying for me?"

"Are you asking me not to?"

"I don't mind if you pray for my well-being," I said, "but I don't want you to pray for my salvation in Catholic terms, or for my conversion to Catholicism. That would be imposing your will on mine, and in my religion, that's seriously offensive."

"I'll bear that in mind," he said. "Don't worry – I'm not praying that you'll become Catholic. As far as I can tell, your soul doesn't need saving, not by my savior, anyway. Not that I'd be disappointed if you chose to convert."

"I hope you won't be disappointed that I won't."

"No," he said.

"Will you let me know if you hear anything, down the road I mean, about Bonnie?"

"If I hear that she's fine, sure," he said. "If she doesn't mind my telling you, that is. She has your number, though, doesn't she?"

"Yes, and so does Family Help. But she doesn't have a phone of her own, so ...."

"There might be something I could do about that," he said. "She needs a phone to keep in touch."

"You're a saint," I said, and then thought maybe that wasn't quite appropriate.

"Pretty sure God and I would both be surprised if that were true," he said cheerfully. "But I do have good role models. I'll call Family Help right now, and talk to you later, Seelie."

"Thanks, Father," I said, and we disconnected.

TWENTY-FIVE

Like most people, I am not a fan of getting phone calls after I've gone to bed.

Too often, those calls are to pass along bad news. Even if they're a wrong number or a friend who's forgotten about time zones, just calling to chat, it takes a while for adrenalin to subside so I can go back to sleep.

This call was not really bad news, nor a wrong number, and it was from the same time zone. It was Bonnie.

Father Michael had organized a cell phone with basic service for her. If she needed anything while she was at Family Help, or after she left there, she could call him at any hour of the day or night. Apparently he'd told her she could call me at any hour, too.

This particular hour was three in the morning. I kind of wished I'd had the phone in the bedroom, but I plug it in at night, and the pair of USB ports in there are over the bed. Not a fan of wires in my face when I'm trying to sleep, either.

"Seelie? It's Bonnie. I'm really sorry to call you so late ... early ...."

"Are you okay? Do you need me to come and get you?"

"No, no, I'm okay, but ... I just don't know who else to talk to about this."

I hoped it wasn't something about her pregnancy, because I had no experience to share with her about that. "About ...?"

"I'm hearing a voice in my head," she said, almost whispering. "If I tell anybody here, I'm afraid they'll say I'm crazy, and kick me out, or send me somewhere for crazy people." There was a catch in her soft voice.

"I don't think you're crazy, Bonnie, and I am definitely the right person to call. But can I meet you somewhere tomorrow so we can talk in person?"

We arranged that.

I picked her up a little after eleven the next day, and we went back to Arby's again for another lunch. We even sat in the bed of the truck again. This time is wasn't because we thought they might ask an unwashed teen to leave, but because we wanted our privacy.

"They said a priest called about me." That was the first thing she said when we settled in with our lunches.

"Father Michael," I said, nodding.

"They said he got me the phone." I nodded again. "Is he a friend of yours?"

"Yes," I said, "and he wants to help you, if he can."

"I've heard some pretty bad things about Catholic priests," she said.

"Everybody has. But I don't think he's one of the bad ones. You could even tell him about the voice you're hearing."

"You don't think I'm crazy for that?"

"Nope. I've heard the same voice. So has Father Michael."

That stopped her with her burger half-way to her mouth. For a few seconds she just stared at me. "No way."

"Way," I assured her.

"How is that even possible?" The burger was in her lap now, on its wrapper, and her attention was entirely on me.

"It's the ring I gave you."

"It's a talking ring?"

I laughed. "Bonnie, it's a haunted ring."

"A haunted ring. *I'm* not crazy, then, but *you* are, right?"

"I thought I might be, when I first found it."

"It's a long story, isn't it?"

"Pretty long."

"Tell me."

So I did, although I left out a few details. I didn't think she needed to know everything that Lady Cecelya and I had shared. If Cecelya wanted to say anything, eventually, fine, but I was content to give Bonnie the basics.

"So the ghost in the ring is six hundred years old, and she came all the way from England to tell me to keep my baby?"

"That's the gist of it, yes," I said.

"Wow. It can't be me that's special," she said, thinking aloud. "Is it my baby? Is my baby special?"

Before I could answer, Bonnie's eyes widened. She looked like a deer in the headlights. "I'm hearing her now," she whispered.

"I'm not surprised. What did she say?"

"She said every baby is special. And she said to give you her greetings."

"Hello, my Lady," I said. "She's right, Bonnie. Every baby is special. Your baby is special – and so are you."

"But I don't know anything about having a baby. I didn't even finish high school yet."

The smart-ass part of my brain really wanted to point out that high schools don't teach you anything about having a baby, or caring for an infant, or parenting, but I restrained myself.

"Now she says there are people who can help me if I keep the baby, or I can put it up for adoption." She was having a lot of trouble getting her head around having an antique ghost in her head, talking to her about her pregnancy. "She doesn't want me to have an abortion."

"Are you feeling any morning sickness at all?" I asked, changing the subject completely. I wondered what, if anything, Lady Cecelya would have to offer on that subject. I was tempted to take Bonnie's hand so I could touch the ring and be in on their conversation, but I didn't.

"No. The doctor at Family Help said I might, but I might not. I hope I don't. I hate throwing up." She glanced at the ring, maybe expecting to see Lady Cecelya's image in it. "She said she only felt queasy with hers. Never vomited."

"Well, you might not get that sick, either. Not everybody does, is what I hear."

"Were you ever pregnant?" I didn't answer, and when I gave her a gentle look that let her know I wasn't going to answer, she changed her question. "Did you want to be?"

"Not really," I said. "Did you?"

"Someday," she said. "Not now." She remembered her hamburger and took another bite. Then she said, "You probably think I'm a slut."

I was taken aback. "No," I said. "I don't. Did somebody say you were?"

"My mom," she said.

"I'm sorry. I don't think you're a slut. I don't think having sex is a bad thing ... although obviously, it can have consequences."

"Yeah. Well, bad decision. I'm trying not to hate all men," she added.

"Good," I said. "If somebody hurt you, it wasn't your decision at all. And I don't think you need to hate all men. Or yourself. Or the baby."

"I don't think I hate the baby," she said. "Lady Cecelya says that's good, and that I should have the baby. If I can't care for it, I should let a nice family take it."

"Not bad advice," I said.

"But wouldn't that be hard? Meeting the baby and, you know, holding it and smelling it and everything, and then giving it away?"

"I'm sure it would be."

"Lady Cecelya says killing it is even worse."

"I agree with her, if you're healthy enough to carry it and give birth. Any choice you make will be challenging," I said. "But it's your choice."

"What would you do?"

"I don't honestly know," I said. "Now, at my age, I'm not sure I'm any more prepared to be a mother than you are."

"Lady Cecelya says if she had it to do over again, she'd keep the baby. She lost another one, you know."

I nodded. I did know that. At one point, Lady Cecelya thought it was a punishment for her abortion, losing a child she really wanted. I didn't know if she still thought that or not.

"I'll still be your friend, Bonnie, no matter what decision you make. But I need to tell you that I'm leaving soon. I'm going to New Mexico for a while. It's a trip I've been planning for a long time."

Bonnie put her burger down and sighed heavily. "I could still call you?"

"Of course. I'd like to keep in touch."

"You're not bailing on me, not really," she said, as much to herself as to me.

"I'm not bailing on you at all," I said. "These days, friends don't have to live next door. We can call or text – and it's not like I'll never be back to Flagstaff. I don't think this will be the last time we see each other, Bonnie. I certainly don't want it to be."

She surprised me then by leaning in and just hugging me, like a little kid. She almost still was one, and she was facing some very grown-up trials right now. No wonder she needed a hug. It lasted a couple of minutes. I felt my sleeve get wet with her tears.

"Lady Cecelya's going to leave too," she said, very softly, when she sat up again.

"Is she?"

"She's a ghost. She needs to move on. She wants to go to Heaven."

"Maybe," I said, knowing Lady Cecelya could hear me, "God would let her stay here a little longer, just so you won't be alone these next few months. Maybe both of you could talk to Father Michael about that."

"Okay," Bonnie said, and set to finishing her lunch.

TWENTY-SIX

I called Father Michael a day or two later.

"Bonnie called me," I said, "and we had lunch again. She's met Lady Cecelya. Now I think neither one of them are sure about Lady Cecelya moving on right away."

"Bonnie decided to keep the baby," he said, half-asking and half-stating.

"She's going to carry it to term, but I don't know if she'll try to raise it herself or put the baby up for adoption. I hate calling the baby 'it,'" I added.

"Have you spoken with Lady Cecelya?"

"Not directly. But Bonnie was wearing her ring when I took her to lunch and we talked, so I know Lady Cecelya could hear me."

"What did you say?"

"I said that maybe God would let Lady Cecelya stay a little longer, with Bonnie for the next few months. And I suggested that the two of them talk to you about it."

"Bonnie called me," he said. "I'm meeting her tomorrow."

"And what are *you* going to say?"

"I'm not entirely sure," he said. "Lady Cecelya doesn't have to report back to me. She's completed her penance, so what she does next isn't up to me."

"She's forgotten a lot of protocol in the last six hundred years. And she's been worried about Hell that whole time."

"True. And Bonnie, well, she doesn't have many people to talk to, and she doesn't really ... know what her resources are."

"So Lady Cecelya could decide to stay here without – "

"Cancelling out her absolution? Absolutely." He chuckled. "Oddly enough, Bonnie's a stabilizing influence on her, even though she's kind of floating in the wind herself. Caring for her, as much as she can, is getting Lady Cecelya out of her own head, as it were."

"I guess what a pregnant and scared young woman feels hasn't changed all that much in six centuries, even if the circumstances are different."

"Not having to keep a secret like that ... and being able to – "

"Put her bad experience to good use, and save someone else hundreds of years of agony, that's got to be a relief. Maybe she needed more than your absolution, Father," I said.

"A good point," he agreed. "God has forgiven her, but that doesn't mean she's forgiven herself."

"And I think she really cares for Bonnie. Maybe," I said, as it occurred to me, "in a way that she never felt cared for herself."

"From what she's told me, she was a good mother, but then, none of her children sinned the way she did – not as far as she knows, anyway."

"I know about Margaret," I said, hoping to ease his mind in case he slipped and mentioned her. Margaret had sinned, but for all we knew, she'd confessed before she died. "I suppose she expects to see her children – even Margaret - in Heaven," I said.

From my perspective, that idea was a little paradoxical. I believe in reincarnation, so there's always the possibility that people you expect to meet again in the Summerland will already have come back to another life on this plane.

Then again, I thought, my mind wandering off on that tangent as we spoke, maybe the meet-and-greet at the end of the tunnel explained people going faint or feeling funny and finding out later it was just when someone close to them died.

There were certainly plenty of stories about dying souls paying a quick last visit to survivors. That had happened once or twice to me. Maybe it wasn't unreasonable that the living could make a brief visit to the other side to reassure someone who'd just died. I've had a few dreams that could be explained that way ....

"Seelie?"

"Sorry, Father," I said, snapping back to our conversation like an energetic rubber band. "Just thinking about our expectations of the afterlife."

"As should we all," he said. I could hear the grin in his voice. I understood. Once clergy, always clergy.

"Easier for them to find her than her to find them in the crowd," I suggested.

"No doubt. Someday we'll find out for ourselves," he said. I thought he sounded a little wistful.

"Father, you're not hiding some horrible secret yourself, are you? Like, you're dying and don't want anyone to know?"

"What?" That surprised him. "No, no, nothing like that. It's just that I've felt like relatives were saying good-bye after they passed, and had dreams – as everyone does," he added. "It makes me feel a little homesick, I guess, sometimes."

"The Welsh," I said, drawing an odd word out of my well of trivia, "call that *hiraeth*. It's missing a place, maybe a place you've never been. The best translation I've ever heard of it is that it's a longing to be where your spirit lives."

"Hiraeth," he repeated, as if he were saying "ahhh" to a cup of hot cocoa on a snowy day. "That's it exactly. I'm surprised I've never heard that before."

"Maybe you have, and just weren't ready to understand it." Now I was surprised. I don't usually go all priestessy in casual conversation. Maybe it was because I was talking to another cleric, but maybe this wasn't as casual a conversation as I thought it was.

Indeed, it turned out to be my last conversation with Father Michael for a couple of years. We finished up talking about his ideas for helping Bonnie, and my plans for indulging my wanderlust, starting with a trip out to Las Cruces, where I wasn't sure how long I'd stay.

It was pretty country, and there was a lot to see and do, but the KOA there didn't offer bacon for breakfast. Father Michael and I agreed that was a serious lack.

When we hung up, both of us were still laughing. The next morning, I had everything put away and the slides closed by seven. I enjoyed my bacon and hash browns at my site's picnic table, and by seven-thirty I was making careful turns to get out of the campground onto Highway 89, headed for the intersection with I-40 East.

TWENTY-SEVEN
Two Years Later

The next couple of years went by fast. A lot happened, most of it good. I did have to change my plans a little bit, once, and head back into Colorado, to a branch of my dealership for some warranty work, but it was nothing serious.

Obviously, full-timing, I shop for groceries on a regular basis, and I can buy bacon whenever I want to. I try to resist its temptation, though, going back and forth between the advantages of its protein – three or four grams a slice – and the harm its saturated fat can do.

Seelie's Rules of Nutrition (also known as Seelie's Dietary Axioms) hold that bacon at the Flagstaff KOA has much more protein and much less fat than bacon I fry up for myself. I therefore consider the Flagstaff KOA one of my home bases. I don't like to be there when the snow starts – right around Mabon, the Autumn Equinox, I head for Tucson or somewhere else warm - but the Kamp Kitchen is closed by then anyway.

But I missed the guilt-free bacon. That's why I rolled back around to Flag again, according to my travel journal almost two years to the day that I'd left.

Checking my travel journal – most RVers keep one, full-time or not – always sucked me in. It was like looking at old pictures, only with notes and few sketches instead of photos. (I do have photos, but they're on DVDs, not in albums I can flip through.)

Once settled into one of my favorite spots at the Flagstaff KOA – one almost directly across the street from the Kamp Kitchen – I stretched out in a recliner and started re-reading my entries for the last couple of years, telling myself I was looking for the exact date I'd left. I soon had to admit that I was reviewing, so that I could catch Father Michael up when I talked to him.

I was definitely going to talk to him, but I wasn't in any real hurry. I wanted to know if he'd heard from Bonnie, and if he knew how she was doing, and what she'd decided about the baby. But I wanted to remind myself how much else had been going on, what my regular life was really like, before I immersed myself in Bonnie's – and Lady Cecelya's - again.

Not that I'd gotten completely out of that pool.

My journal, half-travelogue and half diary, made it pretty clear that I hadn't gotten all that far away from my experience with Lady Cecelya's ghost.

It wasn't anything I could blame on Marianne, either. She'd sent me the maze-box that had accidentally imprisoned Lady Cecelya's ghost for six hundred years before I freed her. But what happened after I left Lady Cecelya with Bonnie – I startled, realizing I still didn't know her last name – all that was on me.

There wasn't anything inherently wrong about what happened. It was more fate than fault. I've been going to thrift shops my whole adult life, so there wasn't anything suspect about my going to thrift shops wherever I stayed.

I didn't think it was unusual for me to be drawn to the oldest things I found in those shops, either. I still had the box Marianne had sent me, Lady Cecelya's maze-box, and it still had a lock of Lady Cecelya's hair in it. But it was closed now, just a decorative item of sentimental significance, and other than my teddy bear, the only such thing in The Castle.

Now that I was full-timing in a thirty-four-foot fifth-wheel, I didn't buy things I couldn't use, and nine times out of ten, I didn't buy them if I didn't know right away what I'd get rid of to make room for the new thing.

It happens that there's a Savers in Las Cruces, so naturally, I went there. The only thing I saw was a full set, a service for eight, of silver-plate tableware in a pattern I really liked. What I had in my cutlery drawer at The Castle was nice enough, but very plain. This set spoke to my castle theme, and it wasn't too expensive, so I got it.

The Shopping Gods are not an official part of the Wiccan pantheon, but I've half-joked about them for years. They are petty and vengeful, I say, having drawn that conclusion from experience. It informs my prime shopping directive: When I see something I really like, I get it, because if I hesitate and decide later that I want it, it won't be there when I go back.

I was happy to gather up my old silverware and put it in the basket where I keep things I'm taking to the thrift shop. They were in it by themselves because I'd taken with me and donated the stuff I decided to get rid of. I do my very best to keep some of the storage space in The Castle unused, just in case. Just in case what I don't know, but ....

A *guideline* for my shopping, now, is to be very careful about getting anything old enough to be haunted. The new-old silverware was, but I stopped worrying after an uneventful month or so of using it.

What I buy is something I can control. What people give me – like Lady Cecelya's box from Marianne – is beyond my control. Once people know I've named my fiver The Castle, they think I want to collect all things castle-y, and ....

After I left Las Cruces, I headed for Albuquerque, sort of. The KOA I like there is in Bernalillo, or as KOA puts it, Albuquerque North. I like it because there's a brew pub immediately adjacent. I can go there a couple of nights a week, get to know people, and not have to worry about how I get home. I only have to walk across the campground and through a little wooden gate.

Kaktus Brewing has regulars, and for a couple of months I was one of them. It was almost time to think about heading back to Tucson, but I ended up staying a little longer because a couple I met asked me to officiate at their wedding.

As a Wiccan priestess, I can perform legal weddings as well as Wicca's religious rite, called a handfasting. This one was unremarkable. They were full-timers themselves, and wanted something low-key, so they chose to hold their ceremony in the grassy area next to the office.

The staff were thrilled, and so were other campers. I was happy to help, and because it was so easy – they provided everything, and all I had to do was wear my robes and spend a few minutes helping them with their vows – I didn't expect to be paid.

And I wasn't, not with money. But, as many couples do, they gave me a lovely gift. Commonly, gifts are particularly nice household items, or decorative wall-hangings. But they knew I wouldn't have room for anything big, and wouldn't want anything fragile. So they gave me – you guessed it – a small antique box.

It was fitted out with a jewelry insert, one of those velvety things with rolled sections for rings and flat sections for pins and necklaces, and a couple of small sections for earrings. As such, it was very practical. It was heavy enough that it wasn't going to fly off my dresser when I traveled, and very pretty.

It wasn't anything like Lady Cecelya's box, and as it had been modified with the modern jewelry holder, I didn't think anything of it. Oh, I wondered when I got it home what I might be letting myself in for this time, and I asked myself if I would ever learn.

That worry was ungrounded, though. The modernized jewelry box was just that: a jewelry box. I found out later that the jewelry-holding insert was removeable, but there was nothing mysterious or ghostly underneath it. Which is not to say that nothing else caught me unawares.

TWENTY-EIGHT

I used my new-old box for its intended purpose for several months, storing jewelry in it.

One thing about full-timing in a fifth-wheel: you do not want to have too much stuff. You want what you need to have, and a few little luxuries, and maybe Plan B items. But you don't want to have the Plan C, Plan D, and Plan E stuff you might end up collecting in a stick-and-brick.

Your Plan B stuff is different too: maybe an extra battery (if you don't go the generator route), maybe a couple of different jacks, that sort of thing, depending on what you have in the way of a trailer or motorhome. Anyway, my new jewelry box was working quite well for me, and I didn't give it much thought, except occasionally to admire it, for a minute or two.

The only thing it held, other than jewelry, was memories of the handfasting I'd performed for the couple who gave it to me. When I found out that the ring-and-things insert was removeable, I used the space underneath to hold a folded copy of the wedding rite, and a picture or two of it that I'd had printed at the local drug store's photo kiosk.

In the meantime, I acquired a cat. I didn't really mean to, but while I was at the Estes Park KOA, I met some long-termers who befriended a very pregnant kitty. After she queened, they didn't like to put her in a shelter and risk her being separated from her kittens.

When I got there, they had two left. They were going to keep the mother and one kitten, but needed a home for the other one. Enter me, not realizing that saying "Awww, what a sweetie" was volunteering.

"She really is darling, isn't she?" Maggie the Cat Lady said. "And you're in luck – she's the last one to need a home. We're keeping the queen and the little boy."

"Oh, I don't think I ...." Resistance, as it turned out, was futile.

"She comes with her blankie, and a couple of toys, and of course some food. She's had her first shots – we have the records here from the Piñon Veterinary Clinic. She's a little cuddle-bug."

Maggie didn't have to tell me that. Alice – I named the kitten Alice because resistance *was* futile, but I'd heard that the Borg queen's name was Danzek, and I didn't like that, so I called the kitten after the actress – clambered right into my lap, stuck her head under my elbow, and commenced to purring very loudly.

"But I ...."

"We'd be happy to get you a cat box and your first bag of litter," too, Maggie's husband Andy said. "I have to go down to the Petsmart in Longmont for some food and litter for Mamma and Prince this afternoon, so it won't be any trouble."

"But I ...."

"Really?" Maggie looked at me, and I realized it was no good to pretend any longer. I had a cat. I sighed in a sort of satisfied resignation, and Maggie said, "You can take her home right now and let her start getting used to your place. I'll just bring a pie tin with some litter and follow you over."

That was how I got a cat.

I had to go online to one of the RV groups on Facebook for advice about a cat in a fifth-wheel. *RV Tips* was helpful, as were a couple of others.

Where to put the cat box so it was easy for Alice to find and use, easy for me to clean, and not in my or anybody else's way was my first question. I considered several suggestions before I took a cupboard door off and put Alice's box in the space under one of the bed-side "tables."

That left me with no place to put my shoes, so up they went into one of the empty over-the-bed spaces. I had to fasten in a couple of bookends to keep the shoes from sliding all over up there, but that was no big deal.

Alice ended up appropriating the smaller space under the nightstand on the other side for her den, though most of the time she slept on the bed. It all worked out better than I thought it might.

When Andy came back from the Petsmart in Longmont, he gave me a harness and leash for Alice, too. "If you train her now, she'll be fine with it," he said.

I didn't leave for Tucson until she was over the drama-queen phase of adjustment to the harness, flopping on the ground like a basketball player looking for a foul against their opponent. She declared so many times that she just couldn't walk in the harness that I considered getting her a small fainting couch.

She got over it eventually, though, and we took a lot of walks together. Sometimes I carried her across Big Thompson Highway and strolled the path through a meadow that is, to me, anyway, nameless. Alice loved it over there. Butterflies, grasshoppers, long grass, short grass, flowers that moved in the breeze – and she was safe in her harness to explore all of it.

However, I didn't want to get stuck up there in the snow, when passage down the hill to the rest of Colorado (also snowy) could be denied by fierce weather. It wasn't all that long after Alice took over The Castle that it was time to go.

That meant getting a small crate for her, because there was no way I was leaving her in The Castle while we were on the road, and even no-er way I was driving with a cat loose in the cab. I folded up her blankie, and tucked her harness in with her, and, very fortunately, she didn't mind riding in the truck.

I seat-belted her little crate into the front seat, and was pleased that she started this and every trip thereafter with a few minutes of talking to me, and then settled down for a nap.

As long a walk as daylight permitted when we got to our new destination, followed by a special Travel Day meal, was all she needed. Those special dinners were her regular kibble, moistened with bone broth. Of course, it didn't take long for her to get me to modify the routine to include a Travel Day breakfast, but I thought it was worth it.

On our way to Tucson, we stopped in Flagstaff for several days. I planned a visit to Savers; there's one in Tucson, too, but it's not as close to the KOA as the one in Flag. Maybe it was just a little sentimental, but I did want to start with the place all cleared out when I got down south. Alice and I were, therefore, going through my closet, and after that, my jewelry box.

One of the rules I've followed for years is that if I haven't worn a thing in a year, I get rid of it. This doesn't really apply to my clothes now, because I don't have that many these days, and I wear what I have. Jewelry's another thing. Especially with the new box, I'd been picking up more pieces than I used on a regular basis.

Wiccan priestesses, I learned when I was new to all of that, are supposed to wear a necklace all the time. I think it's supposed to be literally all the time, but I take mine off at night because otherwise the heavy part slips to the back of my neck and the chain feels like it's strangling me. Anyway, most of my jewelry is priestessly, though now that I'm mostly retired (i.e., don't lead a coven anymore), it's all pretty subtle.

Of course, once I got the place tidied up - not that guests would ever see my closet or jewelry box, or even the pantry shelves - I was going to call Father Michael. My plan was to invite him over for dinner, because I wanted him to meet Alice, and I didn't want to take her to a restaurant.

There are quite a few places in Flagstaff where pets are welcome on restaurant patios, but it's dogs people take, not cats. I didn't think Alice would enjoy a restaurant patio. She'd be able to get quite tangled in her leash, and in her crate, she'd expect to be traveling, and no doubt asking at her surprisingly high volume why we weren't.

A thing about having a cat when you're traveling is that you know that cat toys don't take up much room, and so you are vulnerable to their allure. I took my donations to Savers and came back with a couple more things for Alice – not from the thrift shop, but from the Safeway across the lot.

I had to go there anyway for my weekly grocery shopping. I stuck to my list for food, but the catnip mice just seemed so obvious that I got a little packet of them. They'd take up a very small space in the pantry, and Alice would be at her cutest playing with one when Father Michael came over.

Shopping done, I phoned Our Lady of the Peaks and asked if Father Michael was in that afternoon. He was with a parishioner when I called, but the receptionist remembered me and said she'd have him ring me back when he was free.

He did call, early that afternoon, and we made a date for dinner the next evening. He affirmed that he was not allergic to cats, and told me had something for me from Bonnie.

TWENTY-NINE

I made enchiladas for dinner, some with mild sauce and some with hot, because I know what I like but I wasn't sure what Father Michael would want. Turned out he liked them spicy, too.

He and Alice got along just fine, and he completely understood why I gave her the name I did. She brought him her new toy mouse, and he couldn't resist her either.

When, nestled in his lap, she kept picking it up and dropping it, he looked at me with a *what's up with this?* expression.

"She wants you to throw it for her."

"She plays fetch?"

"A little bit. She'll probably only do it two or three times. Just enough to know you understand and will obey."

He laughed, and threw the mouse. Four times, as it turned out. The last time, she went after it, but didn't bring it back.

"If you try to get it from her, she'll growl," I said, and grinned.

Resistance being futile, he tried it, and got growled at. "Quite the little handful, isn't she," he said, not asking. I nodded. "And completely adorable. I love the one blue eye, one brown eye."

"Me too," I said. "But ... you said you'd heard from Bonnie."

He'd said he had something for me from her, but I didn't want to sound over-eager. Just not dignified at my age, even if my inner child was kind of hopping up and down impatiently.

"Yes," he said, remembering (now that the cat had stopped pestering him). "She came by the parish the other day."

"How's she doing?" My last memory of Bonnie was of a half-discouraged, half-hopeful young woman, facing pregnancy on her own, and not sure where her next meal was coming from, or where she'd sleep once she left the shelter.

I'd given her Lady Cecelya's ring, so at least she had the ghost for company, and of course, she could get in touch with me or Father Michael if she needed anything. She'd called me once, but I hadn't heard from her since I'd left, and I'd been traveling around the two years since then.

"She is doing really well," Father Michael said. "She's joined a teen group at Our Lady, and moved in with a family there. She takes care of their two youngest, and her own." His eyes twinkled as he surprised me with that news.

"I knew she was going to *have* the baby," I said. "But ... she *kept* the baby?"

"She did," he said, playing close with the rest of what I wanted to know. I hadn't remembered him being such a tease.

"And?"

He relented. "And her daughter's name is Cecelya. She's called CeCe, she's almost two, and everybody loves her. Both of them, really.

"She came in with CeCe the other day, and left something for you. I think you'll find it ... interesting."

Since I got Lady Cecelya's box, the word "interesting" has worried me a little. What on earth was this going to be?

He reached into his pocket and pulled out an old-style jewelry box, clearly used. Not another antique, please, I thought. He opened the box himself and took out a silver chain. At the end of it dangled a small piece of amethyst, wrapped in a cage of thin silver wire. He handed the necklace to me.

"Bonnie said that she woke up one morning, and when she went to put on Lady Cecelya's ring, she found it broken. The stone was broken right in half," he said, nodding at the necklace to get me to look at it.

I saw that I was indeed holding half the stone from Lady Cecelya's ring. It hadn't been beveled or anything; the break was clean, and the sheer was visible. I looked back at Father Michael, waiting for him to go on.

"She wasn't sure what to do with it, but she decided to have the two pieces made into necklaces. She has one just like this, and she asked me to keep this one for you. In a house full of children – her family has three older kids as well as the two under five – she thought it would be safer in my office."

"And of course, she didn't know when I'd be back."

"No," he said. "She'd like to see you, though. If you don't mind, I'll ask her to give you a call."

"Of course," I said. "I'd love to see her again – I didn't know if she'd still be in town. And I'd love to meet CeCe, too."

I'm not particularly fond of children, really, but I don't especially dislike them, either. Bonnie's daughter, though, named after my ancestress and me, she was a special child, and I was prepared to be very fond of her.

"What do you think it means?" I asked. "The ring breaking," I clarified.

"Well, it might mean just that it's old and got knocked around accidentally," Father Michael said. "In a house with three young children and two older ones, and a couple of dogs, that's a strong possibility."

"And not all there is to it," I said.

"If I'm honest, no, I don't think it was that, or not just that, anyway. I think it means that Lady Cecelya finally found the courage to move on. I don't think we'll ever hear from her again."

"Bittersweet," I said softly, echoing the way we both felt about that. He nodded. "I have missed her," I said. "I will always miss her, but I am glad she felt safe to move on."

"She stayed – if that's what all this is about – until CeCe was about eighteen months old, so she knew that not only had she completed her penance, but that the baby she saved was thriving."

"It's good to know that Bonnie's found a family, too," I said. I remembered that her father and step-mother, and then her own mother, had all turned her away. "Do you know if she has any contact with her birth family? Do her parents know they have a grandchild?"

"I don't think so," Father Michael said. "After they rejected her, they never showed any interest in finding her. There were no missing person reports. The shelter never got any calls about her, except mine. She's very happy with the family who took her in. She's more an older sister than an au pair, even though they do pay her a little for the work she does.

"And no," he said, guessing what I wanted to ask, "they're not taking advantage of her at all. They helped her get her GED, and she'll be taking classes at Peaks Community College – if they haven't started already."

"Sounds like she and I will have lots to talk about," I said.

"So do you and I," he said. "What have you been up to the last couple of years?"

THIRTY

I had lunch with Bonnie a couple of days later, and of course we went to Arby's – Arby's is our place. She met me there – her adopted mother brought her over. She came by herself. CeCe was at home with their adopted family, and I met her when I took Bonnie home.

"You got the necklace," she said, noticing that I was wearing it.

"It's lovely," I said. I didn't tell her that it was going to be my priestess-necklace forever, or at least until the stone did something else weird. "Thank you."

"I haven't heard from Lady Cecelya since I found the ring broken," she said. "I think she's in Heaven now, with her children."

"I think so too," I said. "And you're with your daughter ... and a whole big family!"

"I met them at Our Lady," she said. "I go there now."

"That's what Father Michael told me," I said. "But he didn't tell me how you met your new family. Or even their names," I added.

"Carl and Tawny Burke," she said. "And Laurel, Philip, Willow, Owen, and Lily – and CeCe. I'm not officially adopted," she went on, "but I'm in the process of changing my last name and CeCe's to Burke anyway."

"That sounds wonderful," I said. "And you're in school?"

"Yes." She sat up a little straighter. "I'm taking psych, and Spanish. But you wanted to know how I met the Burkes," she remembered.

"Of course! Not at a thrift shop, I guess." I grinned, and she laughed with me.

"Carl and Tawny both teach Sunday School, and they're helping me learn enough to be baptized. I don't know if I ever was before, so we're assuming that I wasn't."

I nodded. "Probably wise," I said.

"You're not Catholic." It was almost like she was reminding herself.

"No," I said.

"Father Michael doesn't think you ever will be."

"I don't think so either."

"Why not?"

"Because I follow another faith that I find deeply satisfying and comforting," I said.

"But you don't have churches to go to."

"No, I don't. I used to lead a group, though."

"A coven," she said.

"Yes, that's what we call individual congregations, covens."

"Lady Cecelya said your witchcraft wasn't like hers."

"She was right. Hers was a practice, skills, mostly, that she learned from older women. Mine has some of that, but it's a religion, too, with thealogy and cosmology and understandings about how to behave in the world."

"Father Michael said you're a Wiccan."

"I am," I said.

"You do magic."

"Sometimes, yes."

"Is it like praying?"

This has always been a tough question for me. Over the years, I've tried to figure out how to explain it to people like Bonnie, who are a little bit curious and a little bit worried that Wiccans are doing something anti-Christian.

"In some ways yes, and in some ways no," I said.

"Tell me."

"I will, but I'm curious why you're interested," I said.

"Because of Lady Cecelya," she said, gently, but as if that should have been obvious. "She was a witch, you're a witch, but not like her. She was Catholic, and I think – well, knowing about your religion, that's like knowing the other side of my family."

That took me aback. I figured it was because of Lady Cecelya having to do penance for her witchcraft, and my religion sometimes being called witchcraft. But I was surprised when Bonnie likened learning at least a little about Wicca to learning about the other side of her family.

It wasn't a perspective very many people could take, and I probably couldn't use it to explain to other people who ask, but I liked that she was seeing it that way.

"A lot of people think prayer is just kneeling down and asking God for something," I said. She nodded, a serious look on her face.

"It's more than that," she said. "It's being grateful for what God does for us, and it's thinking about how we can do God's work in the world."

Now it was my turn to nod. "Magic is more than waving a wand or burning incense and chanting a spell," I said. "Prayer can be doing a kindness for someone else, because that's manifesting God's love in the world, right?"

She nodded, and looked thoughtful, so I waited. Finally, she said, "So magic can be doing something nice, too, because that's ...."

"Because that's manifesting the love of the Goddess for everyone and everything," I said.

"But you do make spells."

"Yes. Do you want an example?"

She took a deep breath. "Yes, please."

I like demonstrating. It surprised people, in a good way, and I think it helps them understand. The great thing about people having different religions isn't that they all come down to the same deity, because they don't – at least I don't think so. The great thing is that similar behaviors please so many different deities.

Today we were eating inside. I went and got a packet of salt, and when I got back to our table, I opened it and poured the contents out. I patted it out so it covered more of the surface, and then I traced a five-pointed star, connecting all the points in a single line.

"By Earth, Air, Fire, Water, and Spirit," I said, naming an element at each point of the star. I wasn't whispering, but I was speaking so softly that only Bonnie could hear me. "We are protected from all accident and acrimony." As I said that, I drew a circle around the pentagram. "As I will, so mote it be," I finished.

For a little extra effect, I licked the tip of my right index finger and touched it to the salt, and tasted the two or three grains that stuck. I nodded at Bonnie, letting her know she could do the same if she wanted to. She did.

"That's a protection spell," I said. I swept the salt off the table into my napkin. "And although we don't usually do such things in public, that's the kind of thing we do."

"You don't kill anything."

"Nope," I said. I wanted to scream it. Nooooo! We don't do blood sacrifice. Our Goddess doesn't want any of that. "In one of Wicca's most beautiful liturgical pieces, our Goddess tells us that she asks nothing of sacrifice." I paused. "There are undoubtedly people who call themselves witches who do use blood – pricked from their own fingers, usually – but most Wiccans don't.

"There are people who call themselves Catholic – Christian - but they pray for bad things to happen to other people," Bonnie said. "They're not representing Christ."

"Exactly."

"Lady Cecelya's witches, they'd kill people if they had to. If they could. They usually couldn't, but they knew how and they wanted to."

"Some of them. When Lady Cecelya was alive, there weren't a lot of ways for people to defend themselves against corrupt rulers. They sometimes felt they had to kill them to change anything."

"Now we vote," Bonnie said, shaking her head a little. She looked up at me. "I'll be able to vote in twenty-twenty," she said. "CeCe will be able to vote in twenty-thirty-seven."

"I am so glad you know that," I said. "Voting is a kind of magic," I added, at the same time that she said, "Voting is a kind of prayer."

We laughed and finished our lunches. Now that we had answered each other's most urgent questions, Bonnie couldn't help telling me all about her birth experience, and how precious and beautiful and frustrating CeCe was.

THIRTY-ONE

My time in Flagstaff was wonderful, as it always is.

But it was getting to be time to head south, so I made my farewells, and one morning pulled out to start what was for me a six-hour trip.

Alice was fine in her crate, and chatted with me for the first few miles. Once we got onto I-17, headed south toward Phoenix, she curled up and went right to sleep.

I knew this wouldn't last much longer. Alice weighed well over two pounds now, and was almost five months old, so getting her spayed was at the top of my list of things to do once we got settled in Tucson. I called the Ajo Veterinary Clinic and made an appointment the same afternoon we pulled in.

As a child, I had a cat that my parents didn't know needed to be spayed before she went into her first heat. In my dreams, I still heard her yowling, and saw her scraping her poor little bottom across the floor. I wasn't going to put Alice - or myself - through that.

Once I'd dropped Alice off at the vet's, I went to the nearest Post Office, on West Valencia, and bought some stamps. They were expensive now, but I didn't write to very many people on paper, and post card stamps were still a little less than the ones for envelopes.

The Castle Ghosts   Ashleen O'Gaea

At the grocery store on the way home, I and bought a few things, including half-a-dozen post cards to send to those people who might mail things to me. Most of them knew I'd be in Tucson for three or four months, but I thought I'd let them know I was here now, and also maybe gloat a little to those who were wintering in snow.

I picked up a box of holiday cards, too. Marianne was one of about three people I exchanged cards with, so the box I got would last me at least until Bonnie was eligible to vote.

Alice would be back the next day, with one of those inflatable collars that would make her look Elizabethan while keeping her from bothering her stitches. Maybe she'd be one of those cute pictures on the Internet, if I remembered to take one and post it.

When I got back, I let them know at the office that my newly-spayed kitty would be coming home the next day, and they made me promise to sneak her in and show them. And then they said they were glad I'd stopped back by, because they had a package for me.

It was from Marianne. I narrowed my eyes at it. The last present she'd sent had been Lady Cecelya's box. I did miss Lady Cecelya, but I didn't think I needed another ghost.

The package was flat, not very thick, and about eighteen by twelve inches. I took it back to The Castle and set it on the table and looked at it for a few minutes, trying to guess what it might be.

Place mats? Too stiff for soft ones, and not a thick enough package for more than one of the hardboard ones they had in England. Then again, there was only me here, most of the time, so maybe .... Maybe a calendar of some kind? A little early for that, but she might be sending a holiday gift early, to give me time to get one back to her in time for Christmas.

I hadn't thought of anything else by the time I got the groceries put away, so I opened a root beer, and then the package.

Why "Ouija board" hadn't been of my guesses I couldn't tell you, but that's what it was. It was a very nice one, too, more colorful than most. It was pretty obviously hand-made, too. I looked for a note with it, but there wasn't one. There was a sticky note with my name and the KOA's address on it, in case the wrapping came off, and other than that, just Marianne's return address on the brown paper.

For some people, getting a Ouija board in the mail would be scary. There are lots of people who think they're a devilish instrument for calling up demons. Most Wiccans I know think they're toys – fair enough, since "talking boards" were introduced as a parlor game in the eighteen-nineties – but most of us also think of them as divination tools.

We don't conjure demons, though. We occasionally want to speak with our belovéd dead, in such a way as they might be able to answer back. Do they work? I think it depends on the intuitive skills of whoever's using them. The thing is, you need two to tango, and two to Ouija.

I was happy to have it, but for me, it was going to be decorative rather than divinatory. I knew a few Wiccans in Tucson, of course, but most of them preferred to read Tarot than to play Ouija.

It was, though, on Britsh-place-mat hardboard, so I thought it was probably part of a set. I wondered if it was just for me, in case I didn't want to show anybody else, or if another one would be coming. Had she sent the planchette separately?

•

As I was about to leave for the vet's to pick Alice up, my phone buzzed to let me know I had a text. It was from Marianne, and that surprised me. It was eight hours later for her time, so it was after ten at night there. But it was Friday, so I wasn't surprised Marianne was up, just surprised that she had a free moment to text.

"Did my package come?"

"Yes," I answered.

"Do you like it?"

"It's pretty."

"You'll have to find your own planchette. It didn't come with one. Sorry."

"Not a problem. Thanks."

"Afternoon there?"

"Yes. Going to vet for cat that's just been spayed."

"You have a cat?"

"Yes."

"Send pix. Gotta go."

I was sure I'd sent pictures of Alice to Marianne. I had definitely posted a few on my Facebook page, but she didn't check hers very often. I scrolled back through our text exchanges and saw that I had not sent any that way. I searched for some and sent them, two at a time, before I left for the vet's.

When I got there, the receptionist asked me to wait and said they'd bring Alice out again in a minute. I don't know whether it was her expression or her tone of voice, but I felt a little prickle of worry. It almost seemed as though my necklace got warm, but it was right over my heart chakra, so I thought it was just my anxiety getting physical.

"Hi there," the vet said. She was holding Alice in her blankie, and Alice was blinking at me, so my worry lessened a bit.

"Hi," I said. "How'd she do?"

"Well, she's fine now," the vet said. Not what I wanted to hear. I mean, the "fine" part is good, but the "now" part, implying that "fine" hasn't always been the case, that ramped my anxiety right back up again.

"What happened?"

"Come back with me, and I'll go over it with you."

That didn't make me feel any better. I followed her back to a treatment room. She sat down next to me and put little wrapped-up Alice in my lap. *That* made me feel better, that and being able to feel Alice purring through the blanket.

"So, what happened? Is she alright?"

"She is. Her vitals are all good, her incision closed well .... She might be a little groggy yet from the anesthesia, but she's alert and she can stand and walk. She's eaten a bit, and ... used the box and all. She's fine."

"But?"

"While she was in surgery, she flat-lined. Just for an instant. It might have been the machine, but ...."

"But you don't think it was. You think she died on the table." I looked at my kitten. She was blinking at me, purring, being adorable, and very much alive.

"Well, yes," the vet said. It didn't seem like embarrassment she was feeling. The "vibe" she was giving off was perplexed. "We have no idea what happened. Her kidney and liver values were normal – and they're normal now. Nothing spiked – her heart just suddenly stopped.

"We got her going again almost immediately. There was no sign of a seizure or anything, and none of the routine tests show anything wrong. It doesn't even look like a reaction to the anesthesia – there are no other signs of that.

"It was almost as if, for just a couple of seconds, she forgot to live. And then she remembered. She's perfectly fine now, and as far as we can tell, perfectly healthy. No heart murmur – nothing. And it wasn't long enough to worry about brain damage."

Forgot to live? It was as if the vet had forgotten she was talking to a pet-owner, and not another vet or a tech. "But she's alright now," I said again.

"She is. Of course, keep an eye on her, and let us know if you notice anything unusual, anything at all that concerns you."

"Oh, I will," I said. "Will she need one of those collars?"

"Some do, some don't," the vet said, relaxing now that she was back on familiar ground. "We have the inflatable ones, and I'll be happy to give you one. Better safe than sorry, till you can see if she's going to bother her incision."

"Will I need to bring her back to get the stitches out?"

"No," Dr. Morales said. "They'll dissolve in a few days."

"Okay, then," I said. "Thank you."

"Thank you. I'll send someone in with the invoice."

I did some breathing exercises while I waited, and by the time I had paid and could take Alice back to the truck, I was calm, and she was wiggling. She talked to me all the way home, and I thought it would be great if I could understand what she was saying.

Alice didn't seem to be mad at me, the way some people imagine their pets are when they get spayed or neutered, but she was a little confused by the pillowy collar I put around her neck. She hadn't paid any attention to her stitches on the way home, but I didn't want to take any chances.

I took it off the next afternoon, and kept an eye on her. She didn't go after her incision at all, so I put the collar away, because it's my little superstition that if I get rid of it, I'll need it again.

THIRTY-TWO

Alice was doing fine.

She continues to be physically fit, what with all the tearing about The Castle she does, and all the walks we take, and I let the vet know. Over the next couple of weeks, our lives settled into a very nice normal.

Right from the beginning I took her on walks around the park. If we go up and down all eleven – twelve? – rows, it's quite a hike, and she's a little cat. I introduced her to the people I was getting to know, told her all about the solar panels, and warned her about the oleander. She seemed to enjoy our afternoons on our space's patio as much as I did.

With a grille over the screen door, I could leave Alice in The Castle, watching people walk their dogs, watching kids heading toward the pool or the playground, while I enjoyed some of the group activities.

Now and then I'd invite a friend or two over and we'd hang out on the patio with a drink, or sharing a mini-potluck dinner. I could bring Alice outside, tie her leash to The Castle's stairs, and she might persuade me or my guests to give her a little tidbit.

Alice's meows didn't sound like words, but her meowing was inflected like English. More than one of my new friends commented on it, and quite a few people carried on conversations with her, just like I did. The way she paid attention, it was easy to imagine she understood every word.

Everybody thinks their pets understand every word they say. Almost every dog-owner I've ever met is sure their Buster or Spot knows what they mean. Understanding is a separate thing, most of them have to explain, than a dog actually doing what you want it to, no matter how carefully you explain. Alice, on the other hand, seemed to cooperate more often than most people think cats do.

One evening I was dining alone, enjoying the last of the sunset turning the Santa Catalinas a warm pinkish purple. I was using the Ouija board Marianne had sent as a place mat, and once I'd eaten and washed my dishes, I left it on the table and went to watch television.

I heard a funny little noise, a very soft sort of shussing. Full-timers are always alert to funny little noises, and so, I have learned, are people with cats. I turned to look. Alice had taken one of her glittery fuzzy balls up on the table, and was batting it around on the place mat.

Nothing to worry about, then. "Are you playing quietly, Alice? Good girl," I said.

She trilled at me. Resistance is futile when she trills at me, so I got up and went over to watch her play. She trilled again, and very carefully, very deliberately, pushed her glitter ball onto the H of the board.

Well, cats do that sometimes. They get some idea in their head, I reminded myself, and do strange things with their toys, putting them in odd places. There was nothing unusual about it, really. It was just very cute.

After a moment, she moved it to the E, and as I watched, trying to convince myself that it was just cute, and just a coincidence, she put it on the L, moved it a little and put it back on the L, and then let it rest on the O.

"Hello to you," I said, very softly, and sat down because I suddenly felt I might not be able to stand up any more.

She reached out and patted my arm, and trilled again.

"No, I'm okay," I said. I was used to talking to her. I did, however, glance back to the recliner, to see if maybe I had dozed off over there, and was just dreaming about sitting at the table with the cat.

"Cat is Alice," she spelled out. "I am Arabella."

●

It took Alice - or Arabella - some little time to spell all that out, and that gave me time to settle into a *here we go again* mood. At this point I didn't know who Arabella was, but it did occur to me that she must have stepped in when Alice "forgot to live" for those few seconds during her spay.

Now my questions were, who was Arabella? and why was she possessing my cat? Secondarily, why *my* cat, and how possessed was Alice, anyway?

"Hello, Arabella. Can you understand me when I speak to ... you and Alice?"

The word YES is printed right on the Ouija board, so she didn't have to spell that out. Delicately, claws in, she rolled the glitter ball to say she could understand me.

"And is Alice still there?"

This time she picked the ball up in her teeth and dropped it back on YES.

"Good. I like Alice, and I wouldn't want anything - anything bad - to happen to her."

"Safe," Arabella spelled out.

"I'm going to go get my notebook," I said, not caring whether she knew I meant the one I'd used with Lady Cecelya, "and then you can tell me who you are, and how you came to be, um, residing in Alice the Borg Queen Cat."

"Yes."

The Ouija board consists of letters, numbers, the words YES, NO, and GOOD BYE; some include the word HELLO, but this one didn't, which is why Arabella had to spell it out. No tone of voice is conveyed, so "talking" to someone through a Ouija board is like talking to a computer voice, without the metallic twang.

"When you speak through Alice, is it harming her?"

"No. Not hurt cat. Cat think play."

That was good to know, and easy to believe. Before long, Arabella had learned, or trained Alice - I'm still not sure how that works - to tap the letters instead of moving a toy around the board. That made things quicker and easier for both of us, but not as efficient as my communications with Lady Cecelya had been.

"Are you always there? Is it ever just Alice, without you?"

"2 kwestuns. No; yes."

This was also good to know, and as far as I can tell, it's still true. Now that I know her better, it's really difficult to think of Arabella curled up in my lap and purring. It was also hard to imagine before I got to know her; but I'm getting ahead of myself again.

It was inconvenient to be back to yes-or-no questions. I'd gotten out of the habit, but at the moment, it was less annoying than waiting for "Arabellice" to spell out a longer response.

"Are you a ghost?"

"Yes."

"Are we related?"

"Yes."

I wondered if I'd be able to find her on an ancestry site. "What's your full name?"

Alice cocked her head – or Arabella cocked Alice's head – and stared as if there were a bug on the board. I wondered what Alice thought she was seeing, and then wondered if Arabella knew. I didn't think it would be helpful to ask another question till she'd told me her name, though.

"I know Arabella," I added. "What's your surname?"

"Montefey," she spelled.

"Thank you. I'm going to take a break now, and until I get back, I'd like you to think about other ways we might communicate."

"Alice needs box." She started spelling before I got up, so I read the message. "What is box." There's no question mark on Ouija boards, and I realized then that there should be.

But Arabella's question raised another one for me. If she was in Alice's head, why was she not seeing what a box was, and understanding what it was for? Surely Alice wasn't thinking in words! So how ...?

Alice hopped down from the table, and though I wondered briefly what Arabella would think about the cat box, how we were related needed to be my focus at the moment. I went to my laptop, opened my favorite look-for-ancestors site, and typed in the ghost's name.

There she was. Born 1602, died 1679. At seventy-seven, she'd lived a little more than twice as long as Lady Cecelya. I traced the line back – it didn't take very long, because I had done a lot of that work already, over the last two or three years – and found that she was not only my great-grand-something or other, but a descendant of Lady Cecelya.

I went back to the table and the board. Alice was sprawled out with a broad ray of sunlight crossing her belly. I petted the very warm fur. Alice opened one eye and then closed it again, and rolled a little further over so I could rub her whole tummy.

"We could let her doze," I said.

Very slowly, one of Alice's back legs reached out and her paw settled on the NO.

"Not a cat person?" I asked Arabella.

The foot lifted and dropped back down on the NO.

"Well, she's family, and you're going to have to treat her with respect. If she wants to doze in the sun, we need to let her. I'll come back when *she* is ready to be awake."

A squeak of complaint came from Alice after that, modulated by a cute little yawn. The squeak might have been Arabella's objection to showing so much consideration to an animal she apparently thought was a mere vessel. But it might have been Alice objecting to our interruption of her nap.

THIRTY-THREE

Ghosts can get over on the living in a lot of ways.

Didn't I know it, but unfortunately for this ghost, I knew Alice's schedule pretty well, so Arabella had to wait until Alice really was ready be up and about.

It didn't take long; they don't call short sleeps "cat naps" for nothing. A long, loud meow alerted me, though I thought it was more likely Arabella signaling than Alice. Alice usually likes to come find me, and then pounce on my toes or the hem of my pants.

Alice looked a little confused to be back on the table, on the Ouija board again. No doubt she had intended to be batting at my teddy bear, or viciously killing one of her toys. I wondered how badly Arabella's insistence was traumatizing the cat. There really had to be another way.

"You seem to be my twelfth great-grandmother," I said. "And we have Baroness Cecelya deHulle in common, a few generations earlier."

"Yes."

"Have you thought of another way for us to communicate?"

"Yes. No."

I thought for a moment. "Do you mean 'maybe'?"

"Yes."

"I have my notebook. I can write down what you spell out."

"Yes." There was a pause while Arabella tried to get Alice's attention back from the hummingbirds at my feeder. Alice was definitely still there, and asserting herself. I was pleased to see it.

I also wanted to know what Arabella thought might work, so I tossed the glitter ball back onto the board, and brought Alice's mind back inside. "Spell away," I told the ghost.

"Spell."

I didn't think she was echoing me. I thought she was being economical with words. "I'd have to do a spell?"

"Yes."

"To do what?"

"Necklace."

"A spell to move you from the cat into this necklace?" I asked, touching the amethyst I now wore virtually all the time.

"Yes."

Really? I guessed it made some sense, the broken piece of stone coming from a ring that had been Lady Cecelya's. She'd been able to get right into my head when I wore her ring. Did I want to give another ghost a backstage pass like that?

I didn't, really, but I was concerned for Alice's well-being, and I did want to be able to communicate more easily. I wouldn't have to wear the necklace all the time, just as I hadn't worn or handled Lady Cecelya's ring all the time. And if I was working a spell to let Arabella into the stone, I could un-work it if I needed to put her out again.

"You want me to come up with that spell?"

"Yes."

"Do you have any suggestions?"

"Yes. No."

"Well? What? I know it's troublesome to spell things out, but I can't read your mind."

"No." There was a pause: the hummingbirds were back. They are territorial birds, and I often wonder why the dominant male doesn't starve to death, seeing as how he seems to spend more time chasing other hummers away than he spends sipping from the feeder.

"Herbs," she spelled. Her movement of the cat's paw was what brought Alice's attention back to the board.

"What herbs?"

"Mallow. Rowan."

"Okay," I said. "I can work with those. It may take a while, so you'll have to be patient."

"Yes. 3-4-0 years."

I couldn't help smiling. "Only a few more weeks, then."

●

It hasn't been three hundred forty years since I've worked with herbs, but it's been quite a while. Even before I started full-timing, I'd been away from that practice for a decade or more. Of course, I still made *some* "potions," like peppermint tea for tummy upsets, but nothing that required weeks, much less months, of preparation.

I knew that roasting dandelion roots, and steeping them for a month or so with brandy and dandelion honey made a good drink for summoning spirits. I didn't want just a temporary connection, so I didn't plan to ingest it. I thought I'd submerge the necklace in it while I did the rest of the spell.

Of course, it would then require hours of work to get the sticky out of the necklace, but .... Then it occurred to me that I could take the amethyst out of the silver wire it was wrapped in, and commission a small rowan-wood box, just large enough to contain it.

Rowan facilitates communication with spirits, while protecting against possession by them. That was exactly what I wanted. All I had left to do was compose a spell that would allow Arabella's ghost to enter the amethyst.

Neither of my antique boxes were made of rowan. I was kind of glad that the one holding my jewelry wasn't; I'd have hated to feel I should take it apart to make a home for the broken gem. It would've been nice if Lady Cecelya's box could have worked, but I really did need rowan-wood.

Arabella had suggested mallow, and that sounded like a good idea too. Mallow's grounding, and, like rowan, helps us communicate with the spirit world. If I had time, I'd mix mallow leaves, some oils, and beeswax, and let them brew in the dark for a couple of months.

I didn't want to take that long, though. If I couldn't find the herbs and oils I needed locally, I'd order them and the beeswax online. The ingredients could be in my kitchen by the end of the week, and I could get started.

Arabella had not given any indication that she was dangerous, but as I said, tone of voice isn't conveyed through a Ouija board. When I "spoke" with Lady Cecelya through her ring, I could almost hear her, almost see her expressions – but that wasn't the case, at least not yet, with Arabella. I had no idea what was going on her head, and was determined to be safe rather than sorry.

I'd get myself some tobacco as well, from the plants, not from the locked cabinets behind convenience store counters. That wasn't for the spell to let Arabella into the amethyst. I'd keep it on hand in case I ever felt a need to break the spell and evict her from the stone.

In the meantime, I got out some salt and did another protection spell, including a couplet forbidding Arabella to lie or mislead. I wasn't sure it would work, but what else was I going to do?

•

While I waited for delivery of my orders, I gave some thought to the words of the spell. It can't be just hocus-pocus and bibbity bobbity. You have to think about what you want to achieve, without being too specific about how it happens, while making it clear that you don't intend – won't tolerate! – harm coming from the manifestation of your will.

I doubted very much that anyone would be hurt by my rehoming Arabella in my necklace. I'd be protected, she'd be safe, and the cat would no longer be caught in the middle. Living, if that's the right word, in the stone had been Arabella's idea in the first place, so I didn't mind giving it a try – and if it worked, it'd be fun to tell Bonnie about it.

What exactly did I want to achieve by this sorcery? Well, I wanted Arabella to move from Alice to the amethyst, permanently. I decided to make an appointment with the vet to get the kitten checked out once Arabella was transferred, so when I'd do the spell depended on when I could get the appointment.

When Arabella asked "When," I had to explain it to her.

"I'm concerned that Alice will suffer when you leave her," I said. "I know it's best in the long run, but you came into her body when she was dead for a few seconds, and I want to make sure she's not going to be dead again when you move to the necklace."

"Not die."

"She did."

"Not now."

Hmmm. "How do you know this, Arabella." I was having a very bad feeling about what she might tell me. "Did you have something to do with her dying during her procedure?"

Cats are hunters, and sneak up on their prey. Once their bodies are close enough, their paws continue the stalk, moving very slowly toward their target. That's the way Arabella moved Alice's paw. It took several seconds, and hesitated more than once. It would've been adorable – if I hadn't known it was Arabella, and if the paw hadn't landed on YES.

"You killed my cat so you could possess her body?"

"Little."

"You only killed her a little bit?"

"Yes. Fine. B fine."

"That is unacceptable behavior, Arabella. You must never do anything like that again."

"Fine. B fine."

I hoped the truth spell I'd cast was working, and went on with my explanation about the timing of the spell to move Arabella into my necklace.

"Normally, Wiccans do spell-work according to the phases of the moon, so normally, I'd cast the spell at night. But I'm going to take Alice to the veterinarian – her doctor – as soon as we're done, so I have to do it according to that schedule instead."

"Soon."

I tapped YES on the board, and went outside. I needed to take a walk and cool down. I didn't think Alice was in any danger at the moment, but I just didn't want to be in the same room with Arabella right then.

THIRTY-FOUR

A lot of spells rhyme, because they're easier to remember that way.

Reading off a piece of paper can get in the way of your concentration when you're doing the work, but that doesn't mean you don't write it out ahead of time. I was struggling to come up with phrases that rhymed and made sense in the circumstances.

> *By the power and grace of the Goddess,*
> *and the God, her lover and son,*
> *and by the strength of the Elements,*
> *and my will, this work be done.*
> *Spirit of Arabella, begone now from my cat*
> *and hie you to this amethyst,*
> *and herefrom, be thereat.*

It wasn't Shakespeare; it wasn't even Ogden Nash. But it made the point. It made me giggle a little, too, which was fine. "Let there be ... mirth and reverence with you," says Wicca's *Charge of the Goddess*. This situation was a little bit scary, and adding some mirth grounded the fear and spun it into confidence.

If I thought of something else before we were ready, I'd substitute it, but with the working only a few days away, I started to memorize this version.

I memorize best by singing, and I do that best in the shower. It took me a few minutes to find a tune that worked for me; I have no idea what tune it was, but it doesn't matter. Once I learn the "song," I can recite it without a tune.

All I needed was Arabella's permission, and in her suggestion of this solution, I had it. She didn't need to be involved in casting the spell, and if she was anything like our common ancestress, I didn't think she should be. But was she Catholic, or Protestant? I didn't think either church, in the seventeenth century, would have approved of any form of witchcraft.

The Inquisition only ended in 1650, when Arabella was forty-eight. Even in England, she'd have grown up at least hearing all the nonsense about witches being able to steal body parts and cause droughts.

Still, doing this magic had been her idea, so I asked if she wanted to participate. Alice's paw moved immediately to NO, and then the kitten, with no idea why, got up, walked around the board, and sat down rather emphatically on NO. I took that for a "no."

Whether Catholic or Protestant, she was balancing on a thin, sharp edge, asking for magic to be done on her behalf. I wouldn't know how she justified that in her mind until she moved into my necklace and - if all went according to plan - we could "talk."

The little rowan-wood box I'd ordered from somebody on Etsy was the last thing to come, and by the time it did, everything else was in order. The appointment for Alice at the vet's was set for seven in the morning, which meant I could do the spell just at dawn. That was almost as good as doing it by moonlight.

I had also debated with myself as to the best moon phase for this work. I finally decided it didn't matter very much. If the moon was waning, that would empower Arabella's going from the cat; if it were full, it would lend power to the whole process; and if it were waxing, it would encourage the ghost's entry into the gemstone.

As it happened, the moon was full the very morning I cast the spell. It was full at some intolerable hour; moon phases are determined nowadays by precise astronomical calculations, and not by astronomy or just looking up. We Wiccans consider the moon to be full for three days, one before and one after the actual date and time. I thought it was a good sign by any reckoning.

This was not magic I wanted to work casually. This spell was cast in a full-on Circle. Neither Alice nor Arabella had ever seen me dress and don my robes and cord, or use my athame to conjure the Circle that is a Wiccan's house of worship.

The only other time I had cast a Circle in The Castle was to bless it and its travels, and all who were its guests. At least I knew there was enough room – if I did my work on the kitchen island rather than on the dining table.

Alice was fascinated. She followed my every move, her eyes wide. I didn't know whether it was the cat or Arabella making little pawing motions as I traced the sign of the five Elements – the pentagram – at each cardinal direction.

Once the sacred space was outlined in all four physical elements, I invited the Goddess and the God to bless it with their element, Spirit. And then I was ready to work.

The first thing I did was take the silver wire off my half of Lady Cecelya's amethyst, so that the stone was free. Then I settled the stone into a very small bowl of the dandelion-root brandy I'd made, to make it welcoming for Arabella.

While the stone was resting there, I threaded the old necklace's silver chain through the bail carved into the box lid. Once again, I admired the craftsmanship. The box was not even an inch long, not quite that wide, and very thin.

I'd sent a picture of the amethyst, with its dimensions, to the carver, so I knew it would fit perfectly. Though I didn't think the woodworking itself would fail, delicate though it was, I was going to glue the box closed once the stone was inside. I didn't want it sliding open by accident. I'd worry about it being permanently closed if I ever needed to open it.

Everything was in readiness. The mallow, muddled with oils and shaped with beeswax into what I meant to be a tiny cradle, complete with rockers, was next to the bowl of magical brandy. Chanting tunelessly, I began my recitation.

As I intoned the first verse of my spell, I took the stone out of the brandy. I paused just long enough to lay it carefully in its mallow cradle before I spoke the second verse. Spontaneously, I breathed into my cupped hands and then turned them palm-down over the cradle, covering the stone with my breath.

I expected to wait at least a minute to see any result, any sign that the spell had worked. Patience is the first skill a priestess learns, and mine is strong in a Circle. To my surprise, the little cradle began rocking almost immediately.

My hands were nowhere near it. As soon as I'd loosed my breath from my hands, I held them up so that my body resembled a long-stemmed goblet, with my elbows bent at shoulder level and my forearms reaching up over my head. My palms were open and up to accept whatever energy the Circle wanted to channel through me.

Alice was on the seat of a chair, watching closely, but not within distance of even her best leap. Her head was cocked and her eyes were wide. The cradle's rocking wasn't any of her doing.

The heat vents in The Castle are near the floor. At one end of the kitchen island, I was standing right in front of one, so I could be sure the furnace wasn't on. No air flow was touching the amethyst in its cradle. That left, as far as I could tell, Arabella.

If she was moving the cradle, she had to have gone into the stone. I took a deep breath and reached out to still the cradle's movement, and then took my hand away again. "Arabella, if that's you, please rock the cradle again."

She did.

THIRTY-FIVE

I always expect my magics to work. I just don't always expect them to work so ... so magically.

Then again, most of the magic I do is for mundane goals that I can't achieve through my own efforts, like finding the exact truck and fifth-wheel I wanted. Doing a spell one night and seeing your truck in the classifieds the next morning, that's not nearly so wave-the-wand and >*poof*< as Arabella rocking the cradle was.

Still, I managed to maintain my composure and finish the ritual. I moved the half-stone into its rowan crate, closed it, and set the new necklace back in the cradle. Later, I'd rinse the brandy off the stone, put it back in its new rowan setting, and secure the lid.

But before I could get ready to take Alice to the vet, I needed to thank the Goddess and God for their support, bid the Quarters farewell, and close the Circle. Back when I had a house with a yard, I didn't always close my Circles. I could let the energy dissipate back into the earth in its own time. But magical vibes would be too distracting in The Castle, so I returned the energy I'd raised back to the Universe on the spot.

I left the new necklace in the mallow cradle while Alice and I were gone to the vet. The kitten was quite chatty on the way there – it wasn't a long drive – and looked very good to the vet. Her incision was perfect, almost healed, and she hadn't bothered it at all. We'd have to wait a couple of days for the blood work to come back, but Dr. Morales wasn't worried, and neither was I.

When I got back, I told Arabella I was going to rinse the brandy and honey residue off the stone, and then I'd put the necklace on and we could try communicating without the Ouija board. The cradle rocked.

I was of two minds – and not because any of my dead ancestors were in my head. I really wanted to know if Arabella and I would be able to communicate telepathically, as Lady Cecelya and I were. But I really didn't like the idea of yet another ghost being able to read my mind.

Granted, Arabella didn't seem at all confused, or disturbed. So far, it seemed as if she wanted to be here. But without connecting more directly with her, I couldn't be sure – and if she were psychopathic, finding out when we connected would be finding out too late.

My rational mind, though by now convinced that there are such things as ghosts, was not worried that Arabella could do me any harm. I was still troubled by her admission that she had flat-lined Alice to borrow her livingness, but I was encouraged by her apparent contrition, and the vet's being so pleased with how Alice was doing.

My rational mind was all for drying off the stone, getting it back in its container, and putting the new necklace on. Chatting with Arabella in an almost normal way would be great, my rational mind assured me. I could finally get answers to all my questions.

My intuitive mind was of the once burned, twice shy persuasion. What if, what if, what if?

I compromised. I grounded and centered, dried off the stone, put it back in its exquisitely fine container, and held the necklace in my hand. *If she turns out to feel like a maniac*, I promised myself, *I'll bury the stone half-way to Nogales and burn the rowan.*

She did not come across as a maniac. In fact, she had some of the same worries about me, so it took her almost a full minute before she greeted me, tentatively. "Seelie?"

"Arabella."

"This is ... interesting."

"It is. This is how I 'spoke' with Lady Cecelya." She didn't say anything, so I said, "She had no idea she was dead, and she didn't expect to be across the ocean from home. You seem to want to be here. Mean to be here."

"I have met Lady Cecelya," she said.

"Your seventh great-grandmother." I was glad I'd glanced at the family tree once more before starting this conversation.

"Yes. She is content now, and safe. She remembers you."

"That's nice to know," I said. I hoped Arabella would go on, and not make me ask her how and why, if she'd been ... in Heaven? with Lady Cecelya, she contrived to end up back on the mortal plane.

Of course, I'd forgotten she could, more or less, read my mind. I could put my shields up, as they say, but I had to remember to do that.

"It's a long story," she said.

I settled into a recliner and kicked the footrest up. "I've got time," I said.

•

"I was fourteen when William Shakespeare died," she said. "I only met him once."

I nearly choked. Arabella had met William Shakespeare? "Mmm," I said, wanting to show interest but having momentarily lost the use of my intelligence.

"Francis Bacon died when I was twenty-four. I met him more than once." There was a tone in her voice that couldn't have been expressed on the Ouija board. I understood immediately that she wanted me to believe she had slept with Francis Bacon.

"And?" Now I was trying to play it cool. What on earth could this have to do with why Arabella was haunting the here and now?

"He was sixty-five when he died. Of pneumonia. Before he got sick, he was quite lively."

"And what has that to do with why you are a ghost in my necklace in the twenty-first century?"

"I blame the Catholic Church."

I shook my head. I was getting a distinct feeling of déjà vu now, and I must admit, I didn't like it very well. "Explain, please." I wondered briefly if I should call Father Michael. I had no doubt he'd be interested.

"When he died, I confessed my sins, said my decades, and carried on. I ran into Chris Marlowe in France. He showed me his scar from a stab wound, and one thing led to another ...."

She paused, and I had the distinct impression she was reliving happy memories. Unrepentently happy memories. Her smile threatened to burst forth onto my face.

"Penance?"

"Naturally," she said.

"Can you get to the point?"

"I was seventy-seven when I died. I spent another fifty or so years sinning and confessing after Chris died. There were a few priests who heard more than one of my confessions, and a few who wanted to give me more to confess."

"But you weren't a bawd," I said.

"I never got paid," she said. "I was given things, but never money." She seemed to chuckle at that, and I was not surprised. Double-entendres were as popular in her day, maybe more, as they are now.

"But why are you here?"

"In your ... Castle? It's not a real castle, you know."

"In my castle, and here in my time. Why are you not in Purgatory?"

She hesitated slightly before she answered. "I am. I asked for a transfer."

"I have never heard of a such a thing!" I'd done quite a bit of research when Lady Cecelya was with me, and knew a fair amount about the Catholic notion of the afterlife. Asking for a transfer was definitely not an option.

"Well, that's a figure of speech," she said, sounding just a little haughty.

"Put it another way, Arabella. You know you can't lie to me, or mislead me on purpose."

"I know," she said. "I can't, and I'm not trying to. I just thought you knew more ...." She started again. "I thought you'd be able to follow my thinking better."

"Now you know I can't," I said. I was annoyed. I was out of practice at wit-sparring with ghosts.

"Sinning, confessing, saying my Hail Marys for fifty years, and never changing a thing about my life," she said, in that expectant tone that was meant to encourage me to figure out what she meant.

"Your Catholicism was not sincere."

"No, it was not. It was social. You know your history," she said, now sounding like a sympathetic teacher. "We had the Civil War, in which the Catholics and all the Protestants made asses of themselves, and we had newspapers, so everybody knew what was going on.

"And then there was the Plague," she said, with a shudder in her voice. "I did survive, but I had to leave London, and I never went back. Country idylls weren't as exciting," she said, and I could almost feel her wink. Arabella's apple had fallen quite a way from Lady Cecelya's tree.

"So," I said not really wanting to hear any more details, "the Catholics' Heaven is not your final destination. How did you meet Lady Cecelya, then?" I did *not* want to hear that Lady Cecelya hadn't made it to her afterlife of choice.

"Well, that's the point, isn't it?" she asked, not waiting for me to mention Lady Cecelya's aspirations to Heaven. "The afterlife *is* a choice, and all choices require recompense. For people like Lady Granny Cecelya, Heaven's price is worth it. Not

The Castle Ghosts   Ashleen O'Gaea

for me, but ... I'm a ghost. I can go where I please, and to meet Lady Cecelya, I pleased to go to Heaven. Briefly."

Carefully, as if I was fully aware of what I was doing, I set the necklace down. We hadn't been in contact very long, so she couldn't invade my thoughts if I wasn't touching our charm. I do consider myself fairly well-read, at least, in matters of religious philosophy, but it had never, ever occurred to me that a ghost could haunt heaven without a Pearly Gates Pass.

THIRTY-SIX

As a Wiccan, I don't believe in Heaven, or Hell, or Purgatory.

None of those places is where I expect to go when I die. The experience my religion, my belief, predicts is of Summerland. Restored to my prime, I'll have time to enjoy old pursuits, and to review my life and make notes, as it were, for the next one.

Do the Wiccan dead come back as ghosts? I suppose we can if we want to – delay leaving this plane for a while, to see something through, be someone's guardian. I think of it as kind of like staying up late to see the end of a movie on television.

Just as I can sing along with my truck's radio and remember the traffic laws, how to drive, and where I'm going all at the same time, I think I can have part of my consciousness in the Summerland and part of it here when I die.

It just hadn't occurred to me that in my afterlife I could visit other people's ideas of the Summerland, like the Christian Heaven, or the Heathen Valhalla. It wasn't an unreasonable idea, just one that blindsided me like a ton of bricks.

Before I picked up that necklace again, and let Arabella go on about meeting Lady Cecelya in a Heaven Arabella didn't personally have an eye to, I need to ground. I could have done of the exercises we do before we cast a Circle, but I wanted something quicker and easier. I wanted a snack.

I came back to the table, still munching a cheese stick. I got a coaster for my soda, and put my hand on the necklace again.

"Are you alright?"

"Yes, thank you, I am," I said. "What you said about – about haunting Heaven to see Lady Cecelya, that just ... I was lapsed," I said, trusting she'd understand that seventeenth-century word for gobsmacked.

"You did not know this was possible?"

"I'd have known it was if I had ever thought of it before," I said. I took a swig of my root beer and said, "That explains how, but not why you chose to haunt me."

"You are still lapsed," she said, with a hint of humor in her tone. "I told you I spoke with Granny Cecelya."

"She told you to come here?"

"She ... remembered you so fondly," Arabella said, "that I started thinking I'd like to get to know you, too."

"So ... no aspirations to move on to another plane?"

"None at all. Not now, anyway. Do you mind? You have gone to a lot of trouble to make me feel welcome here, if I am not, in fact, welcome."

"It isn't that you're not welcome. It's that you were so unexpected."

"I had no way to let you know I planned to visit."

"Other than killing my cat." That still rankled.

"I have apologized for that, and promised that I will do no such thing again." She paused, and then sounded thoughtful. "I could have come and rattled your scullery-ware," she offered.

"That would've been better. I'm quite fond of Alice."

"So am I," Arabella said. "I think she likes me too." She might have wanted to reconsider, though, because at that moment Alice hopped up onto the table, from one of the chairs, and spotted the necklace chain.

"Ahhh!" Arabella's startled cry faded as Alice scooped the chain up, hooking it with her claws, and batted it onto the floor. She took the rowan pendant in her mouth and trotted off with it.

Alice is an odd-colored cat, a sort of lavender roan – almost bluish evenly mixed with white. She's almost the same color as the floor of The Castle, and sometimes hard to see. I have touched her tail with my foot more than once, and heard her howl as if I had dropped a bowling ball on her.

I didn't see exactly where she went, but I knew most of her hiding places. She's a little thief, is Alice, and a hoarder. Once she takes something, she doesn't play with it, at least not where I can see her.

I took my time looking for the Arabella stone, thinking it might be a good idea for her to get a good idea of what life with me – and Alice – would be like. I thought I could get used to her staying, if she could get used to me and my cat and our ways.

"Alice, sweetie," I called, "where did you take Auntie Arabella?" Calling my twelfth great-grandmother's spirit "Auntie" surprised me, but then, she had wakened my subconscious mind, and she'd have to live with that, same as I would.

I heard Alice's little trill, and followed the sound. What I found was delightful. She had brought the necklace to my bedroom, hopped up on the bed – no, climbed up over the bedspread, snagging it in the process - and laid Arabella's new home in the lap of my teddy bear. She was lying down beside it, purring and tucking her head in one of those resistance is futile poses.

I stepped back down the stairs and got my phone, and snapped a picture before the kitten got tired of being cute. The automatic flash didn't bother her, and I saw that she had just gotten tired, period, and was taking a quick nap.

Without disturbing Alice, I picked up the necklace and put it on.

"What happened?" Arabella asked.

"Alice happened," I said. "She thought the necklace was a toy. She brought it into the bedroom, put it on my teddy bear, and fell asleep."

I could feel Arabella considering this. I wondered if she would object to the cat's behavior, and got myself ready to say that turn-about was fair play. But, "What is a 'teddy bear'?" Arabella asked.

Children in Arabella's day didn't have the plush stuffed toys that have been around since the late eighteen hundreds, courtesy of Richard Steiff. Teddy bears, named after Teddy Roosevelt after he was depicted holding a bear cub, have been around since the early nineteen-hundreds. Mine – whose name is, for reasons lost in the mists of toddlerhood, Muppy - isn't quite that old.

I explained that a teddy bear is like a taxidermed animal, but made out of fluffy cloth and softly stuffed, meant to be played with. This, I saw, repaid her for surprising me with the idea of ghosts haunting other people's afterlives. That didn't seem to make us quite even, but I guessed we'd surprise each other many more times if she decided to stay.

It wasn't as awkward to explain who Teddy Roosevelt was.

By the time she woke up a few minutes later, Alice had forgotten all about stealing the necklace, or so I gathered when she didn't look for it. She found it resting on my collarbone when she climbed into my lap later that night.

She touched it lightly a time or two, but made no attempt to carry it off again. As she moved it gently, I felt the silver chain itching, and thought maybe I'd replace it with a leather thread. I thought that would look better with the rowan-wood pendant, too.

"So you really will not mind if I settle with you for some time?"

"No, I really won't mind," I said. "Not as long as I don't have to help you with any penance."

"Definitely not," she said. "But tell me, Seelie. What will we be doing next?"

"We will be staying her for a few months," I said. "We will be celebrating Yule with some friends of mine - "

"Yule? Christmas?"

"No, Yule *Yule*," I said, "Mid-Winter. You know I'm a Wiccan - and Wiccan means Pagan."

I felt her energy brighten. "Yule, with a bonfire and a feast?"

"I'm not sure about the bonfire," I said, "but there will certainly be a feast. And people will exchange gifts."

"Will there be snow?" I couldn't tell whether she hoped there would be or hoped there wouldn't.

"Not in town, not here at The Castle," I said.

"Oh." Alright, she was definitely disappointed by that news.

"But we can drive up to Mount Lemmon and see some there. We could even bring some home in the back of the truck."

"I like snow, as long as there is a fire to warm myself by when we come in. And hot mulled wine."

"I'm not a wine-drinker, Arabella," I said. "But we can play in the snow, and then come in and get warm. Look – I have a fireplace!"

I pulled the remote out of the console between the two recliners, and clicked the fireplace on. The noise startled Arabella, but I didn't laugh at her because it startles me too, every time. I gazed at it, silently, for a minute or so, to let her get the effect through my mind.

"It ... it is not a real fire," she whispered in amazement. "This truly is a sorcerous time you live in."

"There are plenty who'd agree with you about that, Arabella, but not on account of something like this. It's electric – it's science," I said.

"Can you turn lead to gold at last?"

"If I could," I said, hoping I was right that she was making a joke, "this would be a proper castle, with stone walls and a moat and all."

She laughed, and it was like hearing Lady Cecelya again. It was pleasant, because I could tell that Arabella was content, not worried, to be here.

An untroubled ghost in The Castle, a purring kitten in my lap, a fire that warmed the room despite being electric – could I want for more?

Well, maybe. I wouldn't mind if there was a bacon wagon at the Tucson KOA, and an easy way to decide how – or whether – to tell Marianne the story about the time she sent me the ghosts of Christmases past, present, and future.

The Castle Ghosts Ashleen O'Gaea

ACKNOWLEDGEMENTS

Thanks to Husband-man, for his unwavering support of my writing (and loud complaints about the computer), and for doing pretty much all of the driving on our trips.

Thanks to my long-time friend CKD for her unwavering support of my writing (and tolerance of my disjointed explanations of my stories as they develop).

Thanks to all our camping friends, who've shared good and better times with us (because with them around, there aren't any bad times).

And thanks to Paige Green, then at Lazy Days in Tucson, for being so patient during the process of finding and buying *our* fifth-wheel; and to the guys who hooked it up to our truck for the first time.

Photo by AO.

ABOUT THE AUTHOR

Ashleen O'Gaea lives in Tucson with her husband and two West Highland White Terriers, Wee Dram and Isla (say it *eye-luh*). With them, she and "Husband-man" road-trip in their Grand Design Reflection 303RLS fifth-wheel to various Highland Games and Celtic Festivals in Arizona, where they hold a booth for their Scottish clan, MacCallum-Malcolm (and are hopeful there'll be post-Covid Games to attend).

Her favorite colors are blues and greens, and she takes her whisky neat.

Find her on the Interwebz at **www.AshleenOGaea.com**. (She's O'Gaea the Writer on Facebook. The dogs have a page, too: Wee Dram the Westie and Sister Isla.)

Photo by Husband-man.

Other Books by Ashleen O'Gaea

O's books are available through Amazon.

There might well be more by the time you read this list.

Non-Fiction

Family Wicca: Practical Paganism for Parents and Children, 2006.
(Originally *The Family Wicca Book*, 1993)

Raising Witches: Teaching the Wiccan Faith to Children, 2002

Celebrating the Seasons of Life: Beltane to Mabon, 2003

Celebrating the Seasons of Life: Samhain to Ostara, 2004

With Carol Garr, *Enchantment Encumbered: The Study and Practice of Wicca in Restricted Environments*, 2009

In the Service of Life: A Wiccan Priestess' Perspective on Death, 2013
(Originally *In the Service of Life: a Wiccan Perspective on Death*, 2003)

Abracadabra for Everyone, 2015   (Originally *The Portable Spell Book*, 2009)

It's All About the Little White Dog, 2014   A history of the West Highland White Terrier

The Boatbuilder's Tale and Other Oregon Memories, 2016   A fisherman's memoir

Fiction

The Green Boy, 2010   First in a stand-alone series about a coven in SE AZ

The Flower Bride, 2010   Second in a stand-alone series about a coven in SE AZ

Maiden, Vampire, Crone, 2010   Third in a stand-alone series about a coven in SE AZ

Mere Mortals' Magic, 2011   A "post Arthurian" fantasy

The Castle Ghosts   Ashleen O'Gaea

The Broken Oath, 2012   Fourth in a stand-alone series about a coven in SE AZ

The Prince Patrick Stories and Other Tales for Children, 2012

Summer's Magic. 2013   Sibs learn about Wicca one summer with Gran

Crystal Witness, 2014   An old necklace helps solve its owner's murder

Quirky: Short Stories and Poems for the Restless Reader, 2016

Fiona's Girl Friday, 2017   A girl copes with her dog's life-threatening disease

The Jollyfoot's Journey, Books 1-4, 2019   Stand-alones in a "space opera" series

Coming Soon

The Evershaw Century, 2020   historical fiction

The MacCallum Charisma, 2020   historical-ish fiction

In the Shadows of Adventure   the Adventure Wicca Book of Shadows